D1758115

One Mistake

Carla Hernandez needs to drop off the glamorous Miami grid. Her aunt's house in Havana seems the perfect place to get over being dumped by her fiancé—and figure out why she keeps messing up her life. But photojournalist Jonah Kane's unexpected presence is one sizzling mistake she's hungry to make.

One Temptation

Jonah thought his favorite Cuban refuge would help him get some badly-needed peace. Still, he's ridden out way worse than the tropical storm trapping him with Carla. And he's going to handle this spoiled little princess on his own dominant, seductive terms just until the storm is over. Too bad this sexy wild card only makes him only want more. And more . . .

No Restraints

Now Carla's back home—but not quite alone. When her baby is born, she's going to raise it on her own, no matter how much she still burns for Jonah. But Jonah can't get over her irrepressible spirit or the passion they shared. And trying to walk away is only making things too hot to resist . . .

Visit us at www.kensingtonbooks.com

Books by Andie J. Christopher

One Night in South Beach
Stroke of Midnight
Dusk Until Dawn
Break of Day

Published by Kensington Publishing Corporation

Break of Day

One Night in South Beach

Andie J. Christopher

LYRICAL PRESS
Kensington Publishing Corp.
www.kensingtonbooks.com

First Electronic Edition: September 2017
eISBN-13: 978-1-5161-0022-4
eISBN-10: 1-5161-0022-0

First Print Edition: September 2017
ISBN-13: 978-1-5161-0024-8
ISBN-10: 1-5161-0024-7

Printed in the United States of America

Thanks, Mom. I love you.

Acknowledgments

First, I'd like to thank my editor, Jennifer Herrington, for loving this story and the Hernandez family enough to help me make them shine and bring them to readers. I'd like to thank the Lyrical team for the gorgeous cover and help with marketing this series.

Cate Hart, thank you for fielding all the frantic, middle-of-the-night emails and for loving my voice. If I could send Dave Grohl to your house to sing you to sleep, I would.

Thank you, Laurel Simmons, for believing in my writing, for your mad copy-editing skills, and for being my friend for over a decade. This book wouldn't exist without Agnes Blum Thompson, Julie Coe, Monica Hogan, and Ann McClellan. Robin Covington, thank you for all the advice, all the support, and all the shirtless dudes who keep me writing. This book brought me to the wonderful women I've met in RWA, WRW, and MRW, for which I am eternally grateful.

Kim and Mark, thank you for hosting me in Miami and introducing me to some of the locations I love so much. Ted Arthur, thank you for being an expert resource on SEAL lingo, gun lingo, and commitment-phobia.

It might seem to be a little strange to be thanking one's grandmother in the acknowledgments of a very dirty book, but Wilda Rose Manka was not just any grandma. She would have read the book and offered notes on the dirty bits. And she would have made sure that all her friends bought a copy. I still miss you. Molly, thanks for reading an early draft and being the best cousin/sister/cheerleader ever. Marge and Jean, thanks for always reading, always listening, and always knowing that this would happen. Mom, thanks for not demanding to read an early draft, for everything you do and everything you are.

Chapter 1

Carla's skin was melting. Her cotton romper clung to her melty mess of a body in the heat of August in Cuba. Rivers of mascara ran down her face, and she would shank someone for an afternoon in air-conditioning with a stack of fashion magazines.

I just thought being with a redheaded Cuban girl would be more exciting.

Her ex-fiancé's words echoed in her head for the millionth time since he dumped her and asked for the ring back. She hadn't thought an accountant's wife *needed* to be exciting, but what the fuck did she know about anything anymore?

She smiled at the driver, probably a guy from Tia Lola's street. He'd picked her up at the airport to bring her to the family home. Lola's house was a couple of blocks off the stately, crumbling facades along the Malecón. When he'd put her bag in the trunk, she'd tipped him with American money; she'd seen her father do it the last time they'd visited. She clutched her shoulder bag, remembering exactly how much money she had in there. She didn't usually carry around thousands of dollars in cash.

When the car had pulled up to her aunt's house, she tried to give the driver more money. In a few words of rapid Spanish, he refused her and smiled. She grabbed her suitcase out of the trunk, took a deep breath, and walked up to the door.

Even though the exterior needed a whole mess of masonry work, the colonial mansion was still impressive. Carla wasn't sure how it had stayed in the family. She knew that her father's aunt ran a *casa particulare*. She rented out some of the bedrooms to tourists for more money than anyone in Cuba could afford, but she wasn't sure how that was enough to keep the place up—especially since Americans hadn't been able to come here for fun for almost half a century.

That was changing, and Carla was here to help turn her aunt's house into a boutique hotel so that her *tia* could retire and so that her family's home could sustain itself.

When she knocked, she was expecting her sixty-something-year-old great aunt to open the massive, carved, wooden door. Instead, a *giant* stood on the threshold. A bare-chested giant with biceps the size of her head. Her mouth popped open—and went dry to be perfectly honest. She made the mistake of looking down, hoping for more clothing. What she found were thighs, just massive thighs, encased in black boxer briefs.

She was going to find her words, eventually. Right now, she just needed a minute. Her clothes felt even stickier on her body, her makeup more melty, and before she humiliated herself by muttering something like *thiiiighs*, she looked up at his face. That didn't make the humidity situation with respect to her panties any better because he had the most perfect face. And the most perfect smirk to go with the most perfect face she'd ever seen. And to go along with the perfect brown skin and the—gah—muscles. The only thing not perfect about him was the scar that bisected one of his dark eyebrows and the furrow between said eyebrows.

"Seen enough, princess?" The giant's voice resonated to her very marrow, and she nearly shivered with the desire to climb him like a tree. She barely registered that he spoke English with an American accent. She didn't even take exception to the fact that he'd called her "princess." That should hit a sore spot, but she wasn't about to let it. Now that she was single, she needed to store this kind of thing up for her spank-bank.

But she knew it was probably better if she said something sooner or later. Before that drool started from the corner of her mouth and after memorizing the pattern of his chest hair. "Who are you?"

"Who the fuck are you?" He reared back a bit and seemed to pull air with him. That's the only way she could explain following him into the foyer, pushing past his big body without spending too much time trying to cop a feel. Indeed, who the fuck was she, trying to cop a feel of an angry giant? It might be time to admit that she was beyond needing spank-bank material and right in the neighborhood of need-to-get-laid-right-now.

"Where's *Tia* Lola?"

"You mean *Señora* Hernandez?"

"Do you ever answer questions without questions?"

"Only when I get my questions answered, princess."

"Stop calling me that."

"Answer my questions."

She'd had about enough of his bullshit, but she surmised that the best way to get her questions answered was to give him what he wanted. "Okay. No, I haven't seen enough because I've been sleeping with the same guy for three years, and he doesn't look nearly as good as you in boxer briefs. Or at least he didn't before he dumped me." It felt so good to say exactly what was on her mind. With Geoff, she'd always had to watch her words. She took a breath, and continued while he still looked taken aback. "I'm Carla Hernandez. Lola Hernandez is my father's aunt. I'm here to bring her—something." She felt like a drug dealer carrying around this much money, but it was impossible to transfer American money to Lola's bank account in Cuba. She didn't want to say money, because while the giant appeared to be benevolent and had certainly made himself at home here, she couldn't be sure. "Now, who are you?"

"Jonah Kane." Of course he had to have a name that sounded like he looked. He appeared to be wearing boulders under his skin. Of course his name would be hard, like rock. "I'm here working on a book, and I'm renting a room here."

"You're a writer?" she asked, surprised. "I know some writers have crazy rituals to make sure things get done, but leaving the U.S. just to get away from reliable Internet seems extreme."

"I'm a photojournalist."

That piqued her interest, but it seemed past due for him to put his pants on. For one thing, his body was going to give her a heatstroke-related seizure if she was exposed to it any longer. He was so hot it was starting to make her mad. For another thing, she could feel his judgmental glare and didn't like the way he said *princess*—it was an insult disguised as an endearment, and she didn't need that.

"Can you please go put some pants on?"

He leaned one hand on the bannister of the stairway leading to the bedrooms, with a sexy, cocky half-smile on his face. "Why? I thought you were getting a great show?"

Carla wasn't going to rise to the bait of a jerk like that. She'd grown up with two of them—both her father and brother were a handful—so she just pointed upstairs. "Pants now, unbearable ego later."

* * * *

Jonah stomped up the stairs, still cranky from his rude awakening. Mrs. Hernandez had told him her niece was coming for a visit. He wasn't sure what he'd been expecting, but it wasn't the woman who'd showed up at the door.

He'd perked right up when she gave him a slow once over, worrying that he'd have an inconvenient hard-on, one that he couldn't control, for the first time in years. She wasn't his usual type. His last girlfriend—if you could call her that—had been a foreign service officer in Kenya. Shannon spoke multiple languages and could handle a bit of rough in the bedroom—hell, she'd loved a bit of rough. Ultimately, the only place they were compatible was in bed, but she was the kind of woman he'd end up with.

Carla Hernandez was a pretty little pixie sprite who reeked of privilege. He wasn't a big shopper, but it didn't take a genius to guess that her outfit probably cost more than all the furniture in his New York apartment. She showed up from the U.S. in an all-white little suit thingy—like the kind toddlers wore. If that didn't say idiotic rich girl, he wasn't sure what did.

If he'd started in on any of the things he wanted to try with her—pushed her up against the wall and shut up her throaty little cock tease of a voice with his mouth—he'd probably ruin her clothes and maybe crack a rib.

No, the freckled redhead was not his type, but she'd managed to get under his skin in about ten seconds flat, and he hated that. He'd negotiated his way out of getting kidnapped by a terrorist group, and he was having dirty sex fantasies about a woman who would balk at the first hint of a spanking. Maybe he wasn't being fair, but his gut told him that Carla was trouble, that it would be best to stay away. That pert, upturned nose combined with the deep smoky voice might make her sexy as hell, but he didn't have time for a regular girl, much less a princess like her. Make him put on pants. He should have dropped his boxer briefs just to see what she'd have done. He smiled at the idea of shocking her.

When he got back downstairs, she was sitting on one of the old, falling-apart chairs in the room that Lola insisted on serving her tea in every afternoon, even though Jonah preferred beer. But, every afternoon he was there. He sat his ass down anyway and drank tea from the chipped service Lola had inherited from her grandmother.

Carla looked fresh and unconcerned as she pressed the cuff of her shorts flat with her fingertip, as if she was ensuring they were still straight. Like a nervous tick. She'd said she was here to give her aunt *something*, but she hadn't said what that something was. He'd grown fond of Lola, and he didn't want anyone taking advantage of her, including her own family.

"What are you really doing here?" His voice was overly harsh, and she jumped. He was usually careful about how he used his voice and his size, which wasn't necessarily an asset in his line of work. Not many subjects forgot that he was there when he took up so much space.

"I don't see how that's any of your business." She might not see it, but that didn't matter. He wasn't about to let any avaricious relatives get at a woman who'd treated him like a son during the months he'd been in Havana. "But, if you must know, I'm here because Lola needs help updating this place."

Jonah looked around. He could see that, but he still didn't trust that Carla wasn't scheming to get this place out from under Lola and ship her great aunt off to some retirement home/purgatory until the woman kicked it. Jonah didn't trust women with perfectly pleated white shorts or prissy-ass attitudes.

He sat down on the chair opposite her and it creaked in protest. "Doesn't seem like it needs much updating to me."

Carla brushed a large strand of red hair off of her face and behind her shoulder, revealing a swath of milky, freckled skin that make him think of summer. Innocence. When he looked up at her face, her plush lips were twisted into a suppressed smile. She'd caught him checking her out. And now she'd be on some power trip about how he wanted her—which, of course, he didn't.

"It does need updating if she wants to turn this place into a successful B&B once tourism travel completely opens up."

"She's never said anything about wanting to do that." Jonah pulled on his earlobe. "I think this place is charming as is. It's a historical landmark. You're probably wanting to tear out everything nice about the place and put in a one-hundred-thousand-dollar bathroom."

She grimaced. "That's mighty presumptuous of you. And, like I said, this isn't any of your business." She got up on her feet then. Her high heel echoed against the bright, mosaic stone floor. "Where's my aunt?"

"Great aunt."

"I'm well aware of our relationship to each other. Where is she?"

"She's at the park, playing checkers with her friends. She usually comes back around four and makes tea."

She mumbled, "I hope she has rum for the tea." She hefted her carry-on and roller bag and walked out of the room.

He had to fight himself to keep from grabbing her bag and carrying it up the stairs for her. And then he had to fight his hard-on again when she turned around. She might be lean, but her ass was to die for. His heart picked up at the thought of palming it, and an image of her mouth, wide with the shock of taking him inside as he grabbed both half-globes, took him over for a split second. Not even her grumbling something about being a gentleman stopped him from thinking about what she'd look like naked and wanting him.

He did not have time for this shit.

Chapter 2

Carla had never liked being pushed around by a guy—in bed or out. Why did it turn her on when he yelled at her? Jonah Kane was definitely the kind of guy who would push her around. He looked like he'd hold her down and maybe bite. And—surprisingly—she'd like it.

He was nothing like Geoff, and she was pretty sure that was why she was insta-attracted to him. Geoff was mild-mannered and—to be honest—dorky. Carla had liked that about him after the string of fuckboys she'd dated after college. Geoff had listened to her, treated her like what she had to say was important, like her aspirations were worthy. He'd wanted the same things—a home, a social life like her parents had, and lots of babies.

At least, until he hadn't.

So many people—her sister, her brother, her mom—had questioned her choice of fiancé, and she'd blown them off. Marrying Geoff, who'd worked for her father's company, had been the one way she could contribute to its future. Her parents had always made it clear that she was generally a debit on the family ledger, that paying for her to go to college wasn't the same kind of investment that sending her sister and brother to prestigious institutions was. She had no talent for math or any real business sense. She'd given away enough design advice to pay herself a salary for a year, but there wasn't any need. She might not be doing anything to earn her trust fund, but she used it just the same.

Once she got into the bedroom she'd used when visiting Lola with her brother and sister a few years ago, she carefully unpacked her dresses, placing them on hangers in the small wardrobe. If it had just been family, she wouldn't have considered changing her clothes. If Jonah wasn't so—gah—handsome, she would have put on worn-out jeans and hunted for her great aunt's stash of rum before Lola returned from her checkers game. But, because she wanted to feel like she was wearing her armor, she reapplied her makeup and put on a dress before returning downstairs.

Jonah hadn't moved far. His big body was straining the wood fibers of one of the chairs while his arm curled *around* a book. She hadn't put on shoes and loved the feel of the cool stone of the steps against her skin. It was remarkable how cool this old house stayed even without proper air-conditioning. It was well built, and she appreciated that.

Not wearing shoes felt especially like a mistake as she approached Jonah. If he stood up, he'd dwarf her with his size. The idea excited her more than she would ever admit aloud.

She walked through the sitting room to the heavy wood cabinets lining the wall. She opened three before she found what she was looking for. Some ice, a lime, and a glass, and she'd be in business.

"Kind of early to be drinking, isn't it?" She turned to find him right behind her.

She looked over her shoulder at him. "I would say it's a free country, but it's not. Still, the last I heard, the regime did not prohibit drinking before five."

"You're one of those 'ladies who lunch,' aren't you?" Jonah extended his legs out in front of him and crossed his ankles, making his thigh muscles pop out. *Why couldn't she stop thinking about his quad muscles?* They were exceptional, but they weren't even the best-looking thing about him. His face had that covered. "You need to start drinking around noon just to get through your afternoon shopping."

Carla's face heated, and her heart beat faster. She could feel it thumping as she replied. "I don't know who the fuck you think I am, but you have no right to talk to me that way." She adjusted her grip on the rum bottle, ready to bring it into the kitchen. "I'm not sure what I did to piss you off, but you are way out of line."

She lifted her nose and started to walk out of the room. Before she made her escape—and got the last word—he was behind her. He wasn't touching her, but she could feel the heat emanating from his body all the same. She smelled the minty soap he used, worn down by a hint of sweat.

If he wasn't such an asshole, jumping Jonah would be a perfect—and convenient—way to get over Geoff. She could have just gotten right under all of Jonah's glorious muscles. But, for some reason, he'd decided that he hated her on sight. And he was wrong about her. She had a glass of wine at a charity lunch here and there, but, until a few months ago, she'd been rehearsing to be the perfect housewife and mother. She'd done that for a year. She hadn't gone out; she'd always had a home-cooked meal ready when Geoff got home from work. Hell, she'd looked through his Internet search history to find his favorite porn. Although she wasn't a busty blonde, she had enough expensive lingerie to be a less-than-completely-flat-chested redhead if she needed to be.

Still, she had nothing to show for it. Everything she'd been trying to do for the past few years to prove she belonged in her family was worthless. She was worthless. And now this guy wanted to pick at that scab.

"I can talk to you anyway I want, princess." His words came out with gusts of breath that she could have sworn moved the hair at the back of her head.

"Sure you can," she hissed. "But you can't expect me to stay here and listen."

She walked out, ego bruised but her head held high.

* * * *

Jonah clenched and unclenched his fists after she walked out of the room. That little bit of fluff had a steel core, and she was going to drive him all the way crazy. She was his worst nightmare, but he wanted her despite himself.

That's why he'd thrown out those biting words, which he'd immediately regretted. He needed her to stay away from him. And he needed to make sure she wasn't here to hurt Lola. He knew her type—the kind that would do anything or hurt anyone in order to get what she wanted. He might want to fuck her, but she wasn't the kind of girl who would let it go at a fling. No, the pretty, pretty princess would want forever, something he never had any intention of giving anyone.

The front door opened, and Lola came through. "*Hola, mijo.*" She always called him "her son" in Spanish, which warmed a part of him that didn't usually feel the light of day. His own mother had barely been around while he was growing up—too busy working. Maternal concern for anything other than his grades and whether he'd brushed his teeth was foreign to him. "Has Carlita arrived?"

"Yeah, she's in the kitchen." He pointed to the door Carla had just walked through. "I couldn't stop her from getting into the rum."

Lola's laugh was more of a bark. "Be nice to that girl." She shook her finger in the general direction of his face—not very threatening considering she was about four foot nine. "The idiot she was engaged to broke up with her, and she's here for tender, loving care."

"She said she was here to give you something."

Lola had this evil smile that Jonah had learned to fear, and it was on her face now. "That's what she thinks." She shook her head. "My nephew sent her here because she's lost, and I happen to be an expert at helping young people find themselves."

Jonah didn't believe in any of that woo-woo shit. "Whatever."

"You should know. You were floundering when you came here for the first time."

She followed Carla into the kitchen before he could protest. He'd never been lost. He'd always known exactly who he was.

* * * *

"Carla, *mi amor*! Come here this instant and hug me." Carla followed her great aunt's instructions and was immediately wrenched into the woman's embrace. Though Lola was one of the few people in her family smaller than her, she was deceptively strong. "I've missed you."

"I've missed you, too." Her words were muffled by her aunt's fluffy, curly hair.

Lola pushed her away abruptly. "You look terrible. Skinny."

"I was trying to get in shape for my wedding."

"Pfft. If you were trying to get into shape, you would have been eating *ropa vieja* and plantains, putting meat on your bones." Lola pinched her side. "You'll make me one of those mojitos you have on the counter, and we'll put together some dinner."

"I thought you served tea at four?" Carla muddled some fresh mint to fix her aunt a drink.

"I'm running late today because I was hung up with my lover."

Carla was glad she wasn't drinking because she would have choked. "Far be it for me to get in the way of you and your love life."

"Not a love life, Carla. Sex." She'd forgotten how frank Tia Lola could be. Nothing like her much-older sister—Carla's *abuela*. According to family lore, Lola had only been in love with one man—her ex-husband—and he now lived in Miami, near their adult children.

When Carla had come to Cuba for the first time with her father, when she was sixteen, she'd watched Lola get ready for a date. Though Lola was nearing seventy, she'd aged in the mysterious way that French or Italian women did. Carla had marveled at all the potions Lola applied to her face and neck. She'd never forget her great aunt's words. *All of this stuff is bullshit. The best skin cream is an orgasm.* Nobody knew what would come out of her tiny, pocket Venus of a great aunt.

Carla had taken Lola's words to heart during her early twenties. She'd made out with every hot artist, musician, and bartender on South Beach—

always making sure she got hers. No one had intentionally made her feel bad about the one-night stands and flings she'd had before she'd met Geoff; it was all part of her flighty, party-girl image.

But when her brother got divorced, she realized that she was getting further and further away from the life she wanted with every new flirtation. She'd thought that settling down with a steady guy instead of a model who was really a bartender who couldn't be bothered to show up for a real date would improve her life. Instead, she was humiliated and in self-imposed exile in a foreign country—a communist country at that. So no opportunities for retail therapy. She really should have thought this out better.

Lola must have noticed her scrunched-up face because she poked Carla between the eyes. "I know you have lots of fancy fillers and peels in the States, but don't court wrinkles." She clapped her hands and pointed at the ancient refrigerator. "We'll heat up some leftovers, and you'll be too full to be worried."

"That's not how it works, *tia*."

"Of course it is." Lola raised her glass and took a healthy gulp of her mojito. One would think that her diminutive size would make her delicate, but her drinking was certainly hardy.

"Far be it from me to argue."

Lola huffed and started pulling covered plates out of her vintage refrigerator. Shortly after that, there was food on the stove, and smells curled around the kitchen to Carla's nose. Back home, she didn't eat Cuban food often. But whenever she smelled *ropa vieja*, it felt like coming home.

She finished one cocktail and made herself another, after which Lola held out her empty glass. After a mojito and a half, she was truly happy she'd come to Cuba. She needed to get away. Around her deliriously in-love siblings, she felt as though she couldn't get her breath. She didn't begrudge them their happiness, but it hurt so much that she'd done everything the right way, and she still didn't have that.

"You look sad again." Lola pushed two heaping plates of food at her. "Jonah will never pay you any attention if you look constipated."

"I hate to break it to you, but Jonah is not my type."

Lola threw her head back and laughed so hard she coughed and choked. Just when Carla thought she might have to break Lola's ribs to give her CPR, she stopped. "That boy is the type of every single person on earth who likes to have sex with men. If I were even five years younger…"

"You should go for it. Since when do you care about age?" That pit of jealousy that hit her when she said that was crazy; she had no claim on Jonah.

"Pssh." Lola made a dismissive hand motion. "Jonah doesn't need me for that. He needs Mama Lola, not curl-his-toes-in-bed Lola."

Carla wasn't about to touch that. So, she looked at the plates. "Where's yours?"

"I had too much sex to eat." Lola's face looked totally innocent. If Carla didn't know better, she'd think her great aunt was a sweet, gently aged, older lady. Not true. Not true at all.

"That's not a thing, *tia*."

"Just eat dinner with Jonah."

"I don't want to. He doesn't like me."

"He's not stupid, so of course he likes you."

"No. He thinks I'm here to fleece you of your savings and steal the family home out from under you."

"Well, are you?"

"No. I'm here to do some updates so you can charge more money." Carla took a bite of the *ropa vieja*—she refused to moan aloud because it was just food, and she wasn't that deprived of pleasure. Or maybe she was, but she didn't want to admit it out loud.

"What do I need more money for?"

That stopped Carla in her tracks. Lola had a fuller life than she did—a lover, a very good-looking man in the house to look at, and an active social life. All her needs were met. Maybe Carla was here for nothing.

Lola grabbed Carla's shoulders, her bony fingers demanding Carla's full attention. "You're here because you need something to do. And I'm happy to give it to you."

That made Carla feel bad. She'd always felt like a burden to her parents. Hell, her mom had let her redecorate their master bath twice. Although Carla was too proud to borrow money, she'd had less of a qualm about doing work for her parents—even if it wasn't necessary. And now they were pawning her off on her great aunt.

"I don't have to do anything if you don't want me to."

"This place needs sprucing up; I think you're just the one to do it. I'm just not going to charge any more money." Lola winked. "I like my strays."

When they walked into the dining room, Carla was gut-punched again by how attractive Jonah was. He stood with his hands in the pockets of his cargo shorts, a stance that made the muscles of his forearms especially prominent. She imagined them pinning her wrists into a bed while he pounded into her. Sweat broke out onto her upper lip, even more unladylike than the thoughts this man aroused in her.

He seemed oblivious to how hot and bothered he made her. If he was aware, he'd either throw her over his shoulder and run upstairs or—more likely—flee the island.

"One of those plates for me, princess?"

"Uh. Yeah."

Jonah sat in another chair that looked like it had to work hard to take his weight. She'd never been into guys who were so big and broad before. Geoff had been lean, almost to the point of being scrawny. She shook her head. This comparing Geoff and Jonah had to stop. Jonah didn't even like her; they weren't going to have a relationship.

"Yes or no, princess?" He looked pleased with himself.

Carla shoved his plate at him and seated herself as far away as she could, next to Lola. When she looked over at her great aunt, the older woman was stifling laughter.

"It's not funny." Carla kept her voice low.

"What are you doing here, for real?" The room was large, but Jonah's voice bounced off the walls and enveloped her in its gruffness.

"She's here to spruce things up." Lola answered for her.

"You didn't mention it." Jonah's brow furrowed, and it killed Carla, but it made his face even more compelling.

"Since when are you a member of the family, Mr. Kane?" Carla flipped her hair over her shoulder. "This is family business."

"I care about Lola." Jonah stuck his fork into his food so it stood upright, which felt to Carla like a gambit to intimidate her. "That's enough."

"I'm not here to hurt her. I'm not here to hurt anyone." Despite herself, she felt her eyes burn. She didn't have to answer to him, but the way he examined her and found her lacking made her skin itch. She'd never hated someone on sight before—not until now. What made her even angrier was the bone-deep knowledge that she would still have sex with him, even if she wanted to stab him the entire time.

Chapter 3

Jonah didn't know why he couldn't stop poking at her. Women usually found him charming, considered him a delight. Hell, Lola Hernandez had practically adopted him over the past few months. But Lola's great niece got under his skin, and he couldn't help himself but try to make her mad.

Maybe it had something to do with how her cheeks reddened every time he said something to her. It made him wonder if her ass cheeks had freckles. He'd give up the righteously good meal in front of him to find out. And he was a man serious about food.

He didn't even have the excuse of trying to protect Lola from getting screwed over by her own family. If Lola trusted Carla, she was probably right to.

He should apologize, finish his dinner, and go up to his room. But he wanted to irritate the lovely redhead as much as her presence irritated him.

"You said you were working on a book, didn't you?" Carla returned his stare, arching one eyebrow. "You've been hanging out at the house all day. Don't you have to go take pictures or something?"

"I didn't have anything set up today." That was a lie. He'd been planning to go out until Carla showed up. After that, something kept him there. Something redheaded. He wondered if she tasted like strawberries. Or maybe something savory like caviar. Just asking the question in his head made him feel nuts.

He pushed away from the table so abruptly that the heavy wood scraped against the floor. Liquids in glasses sloshed and he felt his skin flush from embarrassment. A familiar feeling due to his size. Until he'd started playing football as a junior in high school, his size had been a disadvantage. It had made kids his own age scared to play with him. Now, seeing the look of horror on Carla's face he was brought right back to being the sophomore in high school with no friends. He hated that, and he projected that hatred back on her.

He grunted an excuse, or what Lola might understand as an excuse, and went upstairs.

* * * *

"He's weird," Carla said. "Are you sure it's safe for you to be alone with him?"

Lola glared at her. "I think he's perfectly wonderful. Sort of like having a pet grizzly around the house."

"Grizzlies like to maul and kill things." They were also hairy, and thinking of hair on Jonah's body rubbing against her skin, rubbing it raw, wasn't likely to drag her mind out of the gutter. Her skin pricked up as though he'd touched her.

Once they'd finished eating, Carla helped Lola with the dishes. Jonah might think she was a spoiled brat, but she had manners. Lola's television didn't have any good channels, so Carla kissed her aunt on both cheeks, feigning tiredness. Maybe she would read. More likely, she would lie in her bed, wondering what Jonah was doing or thinking alone in his room. She'd inevitably ponder his degree of nakedness, which would make her conscious of her own nakedness—little that there would be—and then she'd be right back at the body hair. She should have paid more attention to that and less attention to his thighs when he opened the door. Had she known she would hate him so much, she would have been more critical of his looks. If she'd predicted she wouldn't likely see him naked again, she would have been more fastidious about committing every facet of his physicality to memory.

Jonah's room was to the left of the stairs like hers. Lola had made sure to tell her where Jonah was sleeping, to make sure she knew that she wouldn't be able to avoid him in the mornings. When she walked past, she felt as though the sliver of light reaching from under the door would burn her skin. She hopped over the crack of light between the door and the jamb, careful to only let it graze her leg.

She knew she was being silly, but it amused her, and she wanted to allow herself to be amused. Just for a little bit.

Leaving Miami had allowed her to shed a layer of something she hadn't even realized she was wearing. During her engagement, all of her natural whimsy and sense of adventure had disappeared under a nearly invisible coat of fake perfection. As soon as Geoff had dumped her, her façade had come unzipped down the back. Every day she felt less stymied by the need to be someone she wasn't. Although she sometimes ached with embarrassment and the realization that she would likely see her sister have babies before her, she felt more like herself than she had in ages.

Once she got to her room, she removed her dress and hung it up. The air was still sticky, but the breeze from the open French doors, which overlooked Lola's garden, felt like heaven against her skin. She pulled one of her most luxurious negligees, one she'd planned on wearing on her honeymoon, out of her suitcase and felt it floating against her body.

She stood in front of the French doors, and her thoughts immediately went back to how naked Jonah would be. Would he have his boxer briefs off? Would his skin be pale underneath his underwear, or would he have found a way to sunbathe in the nude? Maybe he just hung out naked in the garden every day when Lola went out for chess or sex or groceries? Perhaps that was why he was so angry when she showed up? He didn't want her interrupting his naked sunbathing time.

The presence of carpenters, electricians, and plumbers would screw up his daily agenda even more. That's probably why he was so mad that she was going to be doing work on the place. It was really the only explanation that made any sense at all. The thought of him naked made heat flow through her veins.

She grabbed one of the books her sister had sent along with her. Unfortunately, it was a romance novel, and she was concerned that she wasn't disciplined enough to not think about having sex with Jonah while reading the steamy parts. Since she couldn't just download something by one of those fussy literary writers who only think terrible sex has artistic merit, she would just have to risk it.

She made herself at home, propped up against the largely collapsed pillows and worn duvet. It appeared that her sister's reading taste tended towards sheiks and secret babies. Not something Carla would ordinarily pick up. Her reading habits had tended more and more toward ludicrous erotic situations as her relationship with Geoff had aged and meandered toward its doomed end.

She particularly liked one featuring a priest and a naughty penitent.

Just thinking about that book had her abdomen going liquid. It also had her wondering if priests could have long hair. After all, Jesus could have rocked a man-bun just as well as Jonah. He actually looked a lot like Jesus. And he'd look great in a crisp black shirt and that white collar. Everyone would want to confess to him. Carla would most certainly get on her knees. All he'd have to do is give her a look that said she didn't feel sorry enough, and she'd drop down on the hard, cold sanctuary floor. She jerked just imagining how it would feel to prostrate herself before Father Jonah.

She had to stop thinking about Jonah in a cassock. First of all, they probably didn't even make them in his size. Any of the factory-issued collars would snap right off his massive neck.

No, it would be better—or at least more realistic—to envision him naked. Thinking of him lying on the bed down the hall, his cock resting on his belly, had her hand creeping into her panties.

If there were a contest for the world's most efficient masturbator, she would have won the title during her second year with Geoff, about six months after he'd stopped being interested in sexing her up. At the time, she'd thought it was a temporary lull. Still, she'd thrown herself into the project of self-pleasure just as she'd thrown herself into interior decorating, and mortuary science before that, and party planning even before that.

And now she was good at it. Her skill and the fact that, despite his plethora of faults, Jonah turned her libido into hyperdrive made sure she was wet and on the verge of coming before she'd even gotten her tongue on him in her fantasy. That wouldn't do.

She wondered if he liked boys, too. Maybe just a little. She'd love to see him kissing that bartender she'd dated for a week right before she'd met Geoff. She'd never had a threesome before, but the idea of Jonah's huge, hard body against Toby's lean, blond surfer's physique worked for her.

The idea really worked because all she needed was a lick of Jonah's cock before settling in to watch. Toby had been all talk about getting her the kind of threesome she'd actually be interested in, but now that dirty talk was paying off. In her fantasy Toby swallowed Jonah's cock while Carla fingered herself. One would think that, in her fantasy, she'd want to be right between them. But she liked Jonah looking at her as if she was an interloper. She liked the idea that he would scowl at her while Toby deep-throated him.

She came when, in her mind, Jonah threw back his head in pleasure. The only time he stopped staring at her through the whole thing.

Chapter 4

"This is not a date." Carla needed to be sure he knew that she didn't *like* like him. She was merely accompanying him to the rooftop bar at the Hotel Saratoga because she wanted to catch the view of the old and new parts of the city. That, and Lola had given Jonah the *look* when he'd said he was going out. One that brooked no objection to Carla tagging along.

Carla had gone along with it because she liked architecture, so sue her. And she wanted to see how they had restored the eighty-five-year-old building. The outside of the hotel was painted mint green, with a colonnade on the bottom floor and balustrades around the two upper floors. The corner of the building was gently curved, like the Flatiron building in New York.

"Of course it isn't, princess." His sarcastic tone said that he saw right through her excuses for going with him.

With a twist of his mouth, he annihilated her justifications. She was definitely out and about with Jonah because she liked looking at him way too much, and she was also kind of curious about his friend. For some reason, it was hard to picture him having buddies. Was he as taciturn and self-righteous with them as he was with her? Was it a female friend? Was she cramping his style—cock blocking him—by coming with?

Given her activities the night before and how much she still wanted to climb all over Jonah, she would definitely be cock blocking him if his buddy was a woman.

They walked into the beautifully restored lobby, and Carla gasped. Though Lola's house wasn't nearly as big, the architects and designers who had restored and updated the interior did exactly what she wanted to do in her great aunt's house.

"Close your mouth," he said. "You'll catch flies."

Carla smiled up at him. "I do that with honey."

"Sure, whatever."

He gestured for her to go up the stairs ahead of him, so she put a wiggle in her step as she ascended toward the rooftop.

"Hurry up."

Carla sniffed at him. "Seen enough?"

* * * *

Jonah would never see enough of Carla's firm, little ass. But he wasn't about to tell her that. He wasn't about to give her any indication that she was anything but an annoyance to him.

Her little gasp when they'd entered the lobby was enough to make him half hard. Any more of her cuteness, anything resembling a sex sound might send him over the fucking edge.

And Charlie was going to eat this shit up with a spoon. If Charlie hadn't kicked in half the seed money for this book project, he wouldn't have agreed to meet the guy for drinks, much less brought Carla along with him. But he didn't like the idea of Carla traipsing the streets of Havana all by her lonesome.

So, he'd just have to grit his teeth and try not to tear his erstwhile friend into tiny pieces while he flirted with Carla. And he'd flirt his rich, smug ass off. Charlie reminded Jonah way too much of his former best friend from college, and there were a lot of good reasons for the "former."

Sure enough, as soon as they got to the roof, Jonah noticed Charlie noticing Carla.

"You brought me a treat?" Charlie's question made Jonah grind his teeth and suppress a growl.

Instead of clocking the guy, Jonah lifted his chin. "More like a white elephant gift." He only said it because he thought Carla was too busy looking at the city to hear his words.

He realized that he was wrong when she punched him in the arm. "Never liken a woman to an elephant. It's bad for your health. If anyone around here is a crappy gift, it's you."

Charlie laughed, and Carla extended her hand. "Carla Hernandez."

Jonah rolled his eyes at both of them. Until Charlie kissed Carla on both cheeks, and his shoulders tensed. He had no right to be upset. She wasn't his girlfriend; she wasn't even his lover. But he *hated* Charlie's lips on her.

"Charlie Laughlin."

"How do you know Little Mary Sunshine over here?" Charlie's eyes got big when Carla asked that question, and he laughed again. So hard he doubled over.

"It's not that funny." Jonah narrowed his eyes at his soon-to-be former friend.

When Charlie caught his breath, he said, "Of course it's funny. No one gives you shit like this. I fucking love it."

Carla sat down in one of the orange chairs bordering the pool. "I'd hardly believe that. He's so easy to give a hard time to." She patted Jonah on the arm, and goose bumps rose on his skin. Carla had him on a leash and she didn't even know it. "You can practically see the steam coming out of his ears."

"Most people are afraid he'll step on them if they piss him off." Charlie had stayed standing. "A mojito? I owe you a drink for the best laugh I've had in ages."

Carla nodded. "I'll let you buy me two. That laugh was worth at least two."

Jonah scowled at Charlie. "Beer."

Charlie winked at both of them. "Maybe I'll see if they have anything on the menu that will pull that stick out of your ass."

When Charlie walked away, Jonah sat in the chair next to Carla's and leaned over into her space. "Stop flirting with him."

"You can't tell me what to do." Something defiant flashed in her eyes, and it made his jeans tighten over his cock. "Why don't you want me flirting with him, huh? Jealous?"

"Why would I be jealous? I'm trying to save him from another messy divorce." Jonah didn't know for a fact that Charlie's divorce was messy, but still.

"Maybe we'd be very happy together. He seems like a nice guy. Unlike some of my recent acquaintances." Carla smiled, but her words still hit him.

She might be right about that, but the thought of Carla happy with his friend made him kind of sick. Shit. Maybe they belonged together. They even had the same first initials.

Jonah didn't say any of that. He just stared at her, looking for some indication that she was joking. He didn't know why he cared. She didn't like him, and it wasn't like they were going to start dating.

But it did matter. Charlie brought their drinks back, and Carla beamed at him. Jonah wanted that light shined on him. He didn't deserve it, not after the way he'd treated her, but he wanted it just the same.

"Why are you here?" Jonah wanted to get this over with, so he could get Carla away from Charlie as soon as possible.

"Can you be nice for like five minutes?" Carla pinched his forearm, which did the same thing to him as all of her other touches—it made blood rush to his dick. It was sick and twisted, and he took a long swallow of beer to calm himself down.

"No, he can't." As usual, Charlie was going to say too much. Jonah held his breath, hoping that his friend wasn't going to lay out why Jonah couldn't have nice things. "Ever since college, he's been a surly asshole."

Jonah took in air, but stared Charlie down, trying to silently communicate a plea for discretion.

"You've known each other since college?"

"Yeah, we were the same year," Jonah answered, hoping he could steer the conversation away from a trip down memory lane. "So, man, what are you doing in Cuba?"

"Vacation." Charlie sat back and took a long drink of his mojito. He looked like a tool drinking through a straw. Normally, Jonah would give him shit about that, but he wanted this excursion to be as short as possible. "And I have a proposal for you."

"Are you secretly in love with him?" Carla piped in, uninvited. He looked at her half-empty glass and color brushing her cheeks, glad that at least she was getting some amusement out of all this. "If you ask him to marry you, can I be in the wedding? I'll give him away."

"If I didn't know you were in a rush to get rid of me before..."

Charlie looked back and forth between them for a long moment, with a smile that, back in college, would have meant a trip to Windsor, Canada, and a killer hangover. Now that they were over twenty-one and didn't have to go over a border to drink, it made the hairs on the back of his neck stand on end.

Charlie looked at him. "What ever did you do to make this glorious creature hate you?"

"I don't hate him." Carla smiled at Charlie again, which had Jonah on the edge of a coronary event. "He's too pretty to hate."

Jonah scoffed and pointed at his friend. "Clearly you have some vision issues." Charlie had always been the best-looking, best-dressed, most well-connected guy that Jonah knew. He could charm the panties off a nun—literally—with barely a wink and a cocky grin.

Carla blessed him with her gaze, and he lost his train of thought. "I can see just fine."

"Should my feelings be hurt?" Charlie asked. He never could stand not being the center of attention. "Do you want to hear stories about Jonah in college? There's plenty of shit to mine there. I mean, clearly he hasn't gotten better with women."

Hearing Charlie talk about college and women in the same sentence set every nerve in Jonah's body on fire. Shame and an intense desire for Carla never to know about his college football career—or why he left—raced through him.

"Tell me more." Carla leaned in, oblivious to the turmoil inside of Jonah.

"No." Jonah gritted his teeth.

"One story, nothing too embarrassing. I promise." Charlie had to know that Jonah was about to explode, but his friend just winked. "I know it's hard to believe, but I was quite the dilettante in college."

"I'd never believe that about you." Carla was fucking cooing over Charlie's poor-little-rich-boy act. Fucking hell.

"Well, I was forever trying to get people into trouble, and Jonah was always keeping them out. That's the pattern of our friendship." Charlie took a sip of his drink. Nothing he said was false, but Charlie didn't need to tell her *why* he was the way he was.. "Anyway, I had arranged a booze cruise on Lake Michigan for Memorial Day. And, in his typical way, Jonah found himself tying back his girlfriend's hair as she barfed in the lake about an hour in. I had to keep him from jumping in and swimming to shore for Dramamine."

"That's sweet. Exactly what the perfect boyfriend would do." Carla's words, even though she was defending him, cut him open. He prayed that Charlie wouldn't tell Carla the whole story. This wasn't how he wanted her to find out; he didn't want her to find out at all. He wanted her to continue thinking he was sweet and go ahead being wrong about him.

"You're a lost cause then." Charlie shook his head and took another long sip of his drink. "Carla, have you ever considered doing television?"

Jonah, relieved at Charlie's insanely short attention span, looked at Carla then, the color in her cheeks intensifying as she looked down into her drink. She shook her head.

"Charlie's a television producer, the family business. Ignore him unless you want *Keeping up with the Hernandezes* to be a thing."

"The last thing I want to do is be on TV."

"I don't do trash reality TV." Charlie had clearly picked up on some tension around Carla as a public figure. "I do mostly educational or competition shows—food, home improvement, travel."

Carla perked up at hearing that. "I am an interior designer."

Charlie pulled out a business card, and handed it to Carla with the kind of flourish and killer smile that Jonah had seen evaporate panties and inhibitions all over the world. "If you ever change your mind."

"Thanks." Carla slipped the card in her purse, and Jonah wanted to dig it out and toss it into the pool. He didn't like the idea of Charlie and Carla even working together. He hated this jealous part of himself. Though he usually avoided it by not getting too involved with anyone, Carla had dug under his skin in record time. "Now, what's your proposal for Jonah?"

Charlie sat back, which made Jonah grip his beer even tighter. "I'm trying to get him on TV, too. I want him to do a travel show."

"Like a hotter, crankier, Anthony Bourdain?" Jonah's skin crawled at the scrutiny from both of them. Carla's eyes lit up, and she looked at him as though she was as attuned to him as he was to her. Charlie's smug look had him wanting to rip his friend's face off. That would actually be a win-win. He'd get to rip a face off, and there would be no more talk of a television show.

"Exactly," Charlie said.

"I'm not interested in doing fluff TV. I told you that last year."

"You weren't listening to me, man." Charlie shook his head. "I don't want to do fluff. And you're the only guy I know who can make himself at home anywhere. Look at you here. You meet new people and get them to trust you, to invite you in."

"I don't trust him." For once, Carla's smart mouth was going to help him.

"Yeah, well most people do." Charlie folded his hands on his knees, and Jonah gripped the arms of the chair. He knew how dangerous Charlie's hard sell could be. "That's why you get such great pictures—it's why they're all covers."

Jonah's insides squirmed under Charlie's look, but he didn't give it away. He wasn't used to praise. It had never made him comfortable during his football-playing days; it wasn't comfortable now. Maybe because his football-playing days had taught him how quickly all the praise could be taken away.

Charlie must have known that he had him anyway. "Just tell me you'll think about it."

Jonah nodded, and his friend stood.

"Leaving so soon?" Carla looked up at him, confused. She wasn't used to Charlie. "I was sort of enjoying you putting the screws to him."

Hearing Carla use the word *screws* had him more excited than it should. Anything about her remotely adjacent to sex had him thinking about getting naked and sweaty with her.

"It was a pleasure meeting you, Carla. But I leave him in your capable hands." Charlie walked off without another word.

Carla looked perplexed. "I don't know that my hands are capable of much with you."

"You irritate the fuck out of me." That might be an overstatement.

She didn't irritate him as much as agitate him and turn him on, but that was just as bad.

"That's not nice." Her big green eyes were glassy, and he wanted to take the words back.

"I know you're not trying, but we're just oil and water." Maybe if he kept reminding himself of that, he wouldn't haul off and kiss her. Maybe he would be able to keep himself under control.

The fact that he wanted to take his comments back and kiss it better did not bode well for his plan to keep her at arm's length.

Chapter 5

Jonah was gone when she got up the next morning. Carla wanted to be thrilled that she wouldn't have to face him after putting him in various compromising positions in her masturbatory fantasies, but she found herself feeling bereft of his mean face and gruff voice.

She'd have to rely on Lola's very strong coffee for thrills today.

But that wasn't to be either. Lola was gone, and there was no trace of coffee. She'd have to leave the house in order to get it. There was only one problem—aside from flying here and drinks with Jonah, she'd sort of been hiding out in her apartment since the breakup.

And now that she was at another place that felt like home, she didn't want to leave. Not on her own. The thought of leaving made her nauseous.

Only the specter of a caffeine withdrawal-induced migraine had her showering and dressing, sunglasses firmly on her face. They were so large, they made her feel like she was in disguise. Back in Miami, even those hadn't been enough to shield her from glares of judgment—both real and imaginary—every time she left the house. But maybe they'd do the trick here.

She'd never been like this before. Always the fun one. Perpetually up for a party. Until Geoff undermined her confidence on the way out the door.

Now, she didn't know who she was anymore. She didn't know who she wanted to be—who she could be—if she wasn't in a relationship. She'd always had a boyfriend. A man to impress, someone to keep her safe.

Once she stepped out, the ocean air and sounds from neighbors, already well into their day, threatened to overwhelm her. Her throat closed up and her pulse raced faster with every step she took away from the house. She'd put on heels, even though it was a terrible decision, because they made her feel confident, and she needed every bit of confidence she could get right now.

But swagger wouldn't keep her from face-planting when her heel caught in one of the cobblestones.

So she walked carefully up the block, several men hanging out in doorways smiling at her and saying lewd things to her in Spanish. Just a few months ago, it might not have bothered her. She might have been able to flash her sparkly engagement ring at them, like a force field. It had been so big, it had chastened even the most brazen catcaller. Either that, or the thought of mugging her distracted them from catcalling. Unconsciously, she'd been using it as a symbol of her own worth. That symbol had come back to bite her the first time she looked down at the thin tan line where the ring had been. Even now that it had faded, she caught herself looking at her left hand like it would tell her where she'd gone wrong.

And even though she could admit that she and Geoff weren't right for each other, she'd thought he'd been solid. They had no heat, nothing going in the bedroom. She'd thought that their genuine affection would grow into something more. So, she'd waited and compromised her passion and excitement about life day-by-day, month-by-month, until there'd been nothing left of her. She didn't know who she was anymore because Geoff had left her with nothing. Worse, she'd abandoned herself.

The unfamiliar sights and sounds and smells gathered around her and made her chest feel tight. She could have sworn there was a coffee shop a few blocks from her aunt's house. But, by the time she'd walked what felt like ten miles in her stupid shoes, she was limping and still un-caffeinated. Panic was closing in, and she was too far from home to just turn back empty-handed.

Then, she looked back and saw the group of guys who'd been talking to her following her. Just what she needed, a pack of admirers. As she moved more slowly, they picked up their pace until they were about ten feet behind her. There was nothing in her stomach, but she felt the bottle of water she'd had lurching around. If she could have just found a coffee shop, she could have waited them out. Now, she needed to get the hell out of here.

She looked around for a taxi, but she'd walked away from the busy streets. Thinking about all of her stupid mistakes, she'd walked off course. She started looking for an open door to a church, a shop, something. After about a half-block, there was an older woman hanging laundry outside of her house.

Carla rushed over, and explained in Spanish—as quickly as she could and without pointing them out—what was going on. The woman gave her a genuine smile Carla trusted, and motioned her into the house. Carla walked straight through to the back of the house and across a tiny garden.

She opened up the garden gate to an alley. There was no sign of the guys who'd talked to her, so she walked out of the garden and finally took in some air.

Her eyes stung, and she squeezed them closed. *Jesus.* What was wrong with her? She imagined Geoff calmly explaining that he knew that she was a nut job underneath the thin veneer of socialite. Of course he had. That's why he'd left her. A tear slipped down her face, which she brushed away.

She leaned against a brick wall, aged and scummy-feeling from disrepair. What she really needed was to get her shit together and get home. If she could just make it out to a busy street, she could find a taxi, but she wasn't ready to take her chances on a busy street yet.

Think of something happy.

Unbidden, Jonah popped into her head. His smirk, the one that told her he thought she was full of shit, pushed back some of the anxiety ripping through her system.

Then she opened her eyes and her distress ramped back up. She hugged herself around the waist and bowed her head, trying to get her breathing back on track. She wished there was someone she could call, but her cell wouldn't work down here. And she didn't want to be the one calling for help anymore. She needed to be the person who picked herself up and dusted herself off.

Carla didn't know how long she stood there. She lost track of time and space, digging deep inside, trying to remember how it felt to be safe.

Blood still rushed past her eardrums, creating a mighty white noise that drowned out the people sounds, the street noise. She gulped down deep, slow breaths until a clicking—the kind a camera shutter made—came close, and she felt the heat of a huge body.

She knew it was Jonah before she opened her eyes. His minty soap was distinct among the rotted food and garbage. Hell, she'd known it was him as soon as she'd heard the first shutter click. Every bit of her was aware of him in a way she hadn't felt in years—maybe ever.

He stopped about a foot from her, but he didn't try to touch her. Of course, he wouldn't. He probably didn't have a sick preoccupation with her like she did him. She could admit that the last two nights' solo fun had been weird and creepy on her part. Still, her lower abdomen tugged inward when she got a smell of his sun- and work-warmed body.

"Breathe." He commanded her, but the word was soft. Like he could *make* her breathe, but he wanted her to do it on her own.

"Trying." Sweat trickled between her breasts. She was sure she made a really attractive picture right now, sweaty and falling apart.

"Can I touch you?"

His words buzzed through her. She opened her eyes then. Seeing him standing there, in a T-shirt he'd probably had for decades and jeans worn to the exact specifications of his enormous quadriceps, she had to stop herself from begging him to touch her.

"You're asking?"

"Of course I'm asking." He ran a hand over his head, bringing the strands of hair that made him look like a jacked-up pirate away from his brow. "Can I touch you?"

"To do what?" Carla huffed out a breath, noting that she wasn't shaking anymore, and she didn't feel like she was going to puke. Progress. "Are you going to pick me up and throw me into the ocean?"

He laughed, and it was the most magical sound on the entire island, maybe in the whole Caribbean Sea right then. His laugh vibrated through her skin. She felt as though she was being washed in his amusement, which was all well and good until she remembered that he was laughing *at* her.

She scowled at him despite her sudden, inexplicable urge to join in his little giggle fest. "I'm serious. You think I'm trying to scam a member of my family. Why wouldn't you want to hurt me?"

He moved closer, so close she could feel his breaths, big breaths, against her cheek. He rested one clenched fist against the wall behind her, leaving her an escape. She wouldn't take it because she wasn't sure she could make herself get out of the shelter his body created right then.

"One." He stuck up the index finger of his free hand. "I have never hurt a woman."

"I believe you." She did. Despite the fact that having her character besmirched irritated her, she didn't think he was an abusive shitbag.

He just ignored her confession, as if it was foregone that she would believe him. "Two." His middle finger went up, and she imagined it slipping between her dress and the skin above her breast. Having him this close and thinking about him touching her was going to make her lose her mind. Not a problem that either of them needed. "I was probably wrong about you."

The words sounded like they'd been wrenched out of him, as though he rarely, if ever, admitted that he made a mistake or misjudged a situation.

"So you don't think I'm a silly, spoiled brat?"

"You *are* a silly, spoiled brat. But you're not trying to rip Lola off." He dropped his hand, and her fantasies about how his blunt fingertips could make her feel fell away as his words sank in.

"What makes you think I'm not? If I'm such a princess, what makes you think I have moral qualms about anything?"

"The way Lola talks about you." His rumbly voice made her skin tingle, in the best way. He was electrifying in all the respects that Geoff had never been, and it made her angry. She wasn't sure why. Wouldn't the breakup have been even worse had she actually been in love with her fiancé? "She talks about you as if you're a wounded bird or something."

She was a wounded animal, but not a bird. Jonah didn't know her well enough to know that she was really a wounded honey badger. And, right now, the feral part of her that ached with not being wanted was fighting its way out of her chest. That bit of wildness that she hadn't completely killed off for Geoff's benefit wondered what he would do if she vaulted up to the very tips of her toes and kissed him. She wanted to feel his huge palms envelop her hips and ass and crush her against him. At the same time, she wanted to scratch her nails against the skin on his back, raising welts and possibly drawing blood.

All of these emotions distracted her from the feelings of shame and anxiety scraping through her guts. Hating Jonah and wanting to fuck him at the same time gave all her angry energy a place to go.

As though he sensed her drawing closer to him, snapping and pressing her lips and body against him, he pulled away. She must repel him on some level.

"Do you need help getting back to the house?"

Carla wanted to say no, but she couldn't. She would just have another freak out if she tried to make it to the house all alone. She hated feeling this vulnerable. Would she always feel like this? Would she need someone to swoop in and save her for the rest of her life?

She chewed on her answer for long seconds before saying, "Yes."

"At your service."

"No, you're not." She coughed up a laugh despite her bone-deep embarrassment. "You're just afraid that I'll tell Lola you abandoned me, and she'll kick you out."

He opened his palms to her and delivered another killer smile. "You've got me there, princess."

"I wish you wouldn't call me that."

"If the shoe fits." He looked down her body to her feet, and back up. Slowly. As if she wasn't repulsive to him at all. She'd recognize the look on his face anywhere, it was hunger. Lust.

Knowing he wanted her body made her own desire for him even hotter. It made her wonder why he didn't want to give in, what was holding him back. Her curiosity reminded her of hiding underneath the dining room table during her mother's lunches. She used to bring down a notepad and write down all the major items of gossip in bullet points. Then, she would brief her father on who was cheating on whom with who so that he wouldn't stick his foot in a pile of doo-doo at the next cocktail party her mom threw.

Her mother had always thought she just wanted to hang out with the big girls. But, even then, she'd wanted to prove that she had value to the family. She hadn't been as good at school as Alana or as good at sports as Javi. But she'd always had the whole mercenary game down pat.

Jonah might only see a flighty, wounded bird who ought to be put out of her misery, but she was not to be underestimated.

That was it! He didn't want her because he only saw the surface. The urge to put him in his place rolled through her body as sure as her unsatisfied sexual longing coursed through her veins. He didn't want her because he didn't really *see* her. And she wanted to make him see her almost as much as she wanted to break down his resistance to her.

"Can you make it back in those?" He pointed at her shoes.

She had to fight a knowing smile because she couldn't be the damsel in distress if he knew that she was playing him so he'd have to carry her back.

So, she shifted from foot to foot, feigning more serious foot pain. "Probably not. I thought there was a coffee place about a block from Lola's. I got lost." A muscle ticked in Jonah's cheek while he hesitated. She poured more gasoline on the fire. "I know you're probably busy taking pictures."

She trailed a finger along his forearm, toward the camera bag clenched in his fist. He continued to hesitate, and it just made this little game all the more fun. He'd pretend to be so put out by her because he had to deviate from his busy schedule. She would pour her gratitude on ever thicker until it made him angry. And then he would get so pissed that he would kiss her.

She wondered if she could make him so mad that he went downtown, just pushed her panties to the side and put his mouth on her. Hashtag: life goals.

With a muttered *"Fuck,"* he hiked his camera bag over his shoulder and scooped her up.

The feel of his hands against her, and his warm chest against the side of her breast were even more affecting than she'd thought. She'd wanted him before. And now, she was on fire for him.

She had a feeling she was playing a game that she could only lose.

* * * *

Jonah had always been a magnet for girls who needed a lot of—attention, love, money, whatever. He liked the feeling of being needed, but the ones who needed him always turned out to be the problems.

Carla had "problem" written all over her delicious little body. But that didn't matter to his dick. His dick's only thoughts on Carla were about how warm and tight she'd be inside and how much his dick liked her. His dick was an asshole.

She weighed about nothing and twenty pounds, but that didn't keep him from resenting the fact that he was carrying a girl through the streets of Havana, *Officer and a Gentleman*-style. Especially with the way her tits bounced with each step—did she ever wear a bra?

He'd been photographing interesting architectural features of buildings in Lola's neighborhood when he saw her nearly collapsed in the alley. As he'd gotten closer, he'd recognized the signs of a panic attack. He'd had them before, but that had been in Syria. He couldn't fucking stand seeing all those children suffering. And, before that, he used to hyperventilate and throw up before every game in college.

He'd taken his first vacation to Cuba after his last time in Syria. Part of the reason he'd started working on the book was to avoid heading back to the Middle East. Havana wasn't sunshine and roses; extreme poverty was everywhere, and people lacked basic civil rights, but there was hope that not everything was broken forever.

Given his history in war zones, he'd known not to touch her or make any sudden movements. He'd expected her to take his help gratefully. She'd surprised him again by joking about him throwing her in the ocean. And her mention of the ocean had him thinking about her in a string bikini.

Wondering if she had freckles everywhere while cradling her to his chest had him nearly stumbling. He couldn't wait to get her back to Lola's and be rid of her for the day.

"We need to stop for coffee."

"What? You want to grab a cup of Joe after that meltdown?" He shook his head. "The last thing you need is coffee, princess."

"Some guys were following me. I was in that alley because I lost them."

Jonah fought the urge to put her down and go find the motherfuckers. He was serious about not hurting women. After the way he'd hurt his college girlfriend—emotionally—he'd vowed never to hurt a woman again. Not if she didn't ask him to.

Instead, he said, "You need me to go back and rearrange some faces more than you need coffee, princess."

"I told you to stop calling me that." She pinched his chest, and it made him laugh. Her tiny little fingers could probably dig in and rip off a nipple if he wasn't careful, but she hadn't hurt him, just opened up a new channel of sensation right to his dick. "I need coffee so I don't get a migraine."

"Your caffeine addiction is so serious that you'll risk being chased down by dudes and having a panic attack in an unfamiliar city just to avoid a headache."

"Was that what that was? I thought I was having a heart attack for a few minutes."

He had so many questions, but he wasn't great with the talking. He was much better with pictures. Why did she have her first panic attack then? Was it just those guys? Or was she having a nervous breakdown about her breakup? Why was she a wounded bird? And why did she have the same effect as a bottle of Viagra? He didn't ask any of those questions. He simply said, "Whatever, princess. I'm not stopping for coffee."

"But I need my fix. Haven't you spent enough time in Cuba to realize that *cafecito* is life?" He winced at her whiny exclamation. She was a no-joke, seriously spoiled brat, and it grated on his nerves even more now that he'd decided to take on a knight-in-shining-armor gig on her behalf. "I'll get a migraine."

She bucked against him, and he almost dropped her.

"Suck it up, buttercup."

"I like that even less than the other nickname."

"How about I just call you 'Princess Buttercup,' so you can really hate me." She giggled, and it was cloyingly sweet, the kind of sweet that hit all the pleasure receptors in his brain and would, for sure, give him a sugar coma later.

"As you wish." She stopped wiggling—finally—and rested her head on his shoulder. "Just as long as I can call you 'Westley.'"

The fuck she would. He wasn't some dopey Prince Charming, ready and willing to ride in and save anyone. Hell, he could barely save himself half the time. He might go into war zones and conflict areas on a routine basis, but he was just as vulnerable and liable to get his ass blown up as the next guy. He'd been luckier in his work than he ever had been in his personal life. That's why it was best to stick to women like Shannon. Self-sufficient. Competent. Women who didn't wear heels.

"Who's the bad guy in that movie?" She'd relaxed once they'd started talking about *The Princess Bride*. His mom loved that movie, and he'd seen it a million times, but he wanted to keep her talking about something other than stopping for coffee. And he wanted her to think about something other than the fact that they were making a bit of a spectacle on the street.

Several old ladies had clapped their hands together and cocked their heads in the universal symbol of "*Awww, what a cute couple.*"

"I don't remember. No one ever remembers the bad guy."

In his experience, nothing could be further from the truth. People still remembered the one bad thing he'd done. The only reason Carla didn't know—the only reason she was treating him like he really could be her hero right now—was that she didn't have the luxury of a Google search at her fingertips.

He should just tell her so that she'd stay clear of him. She wouldn't be looking at him right now like she wanted to kiss him. She'd probably slap him across the face or give him the cold shoulder. Even after knowing her for less than twenty-four hours, he knew that the silent treatment from Carla Hernandez would cut him.

So, he'd keep her talking about normal-people things like movies. That way, when she went back to Miami, she'd search him on the Internet one day and she could hate him. He'd be rid of her forever. He wasn't sure why he hated that thought.

"People remember the winners," she said. "And sometimes the losers if the losers lose in a truly spectacular fashion."

"You're not a loser, princess." He didn't know why he said that, but she was vulnerable right now because of the loser fiancé. He also wasn't sure when he'd started thinking of the fiancé as a loser, but he had to be if someone as sweet and soft as Carla was this broken up about him. If he had her in his bed and gave it up, he was a stupid loser. She must have really loved him, which proved that she was sweet and soft but not for him.

"Well, I lost my parents' deposits on the wedding."

"Better than getting married and divorced."

"How do you know? Have you ever been married?"

He wasn't sure how to answer the question. If he was smart, he'd say yes. But then he'd have to explain a whole bunch of shit he didn't want to explain. Like how he had never actually gotten married. He'd offered to marry a girl who didn't want him, who hadn't wanted to live. So, he just grunted. And he couldn't help it if she interpreted his grunt as an answer.

"So, then you don't know." She looked away from him, which almost tipped them both over from the shift in balance. Her clasp around his neck tightened. "It could have worked out if he had just wanted to try."

He adjusted her weight in his arms. "Sometimes people are shit at trying."

Jonah didn't know why he was trying to comfort her. He didn't care about her feelings. Caring about feelings got him in trouble once, and he didn't want trouble.

When they got back to the house, Carla stayed nestled against him, and he didn't feel the need to put her down right away. She felt nice there, and he knew she'd do something annoying in a few minutes to remind him why he stayed away from high-maintenance women.

She wiggled when his pause became awkward, and it didn't make him want to let her go. It made him hard. He needed to go inside and take a cold shower so he and his dick could be alone.

He very carefully placed her on her feet inside the door. Fairy light, she walked up the stairs in front of him, tightening his jeans even more. The muscles of her smooth calves flexed and pulsed with each step. Her proportionally generous hips swayed back and forth, hypnotizing him.

She shocked him when she looked over her shoulder and said, "Seen enough?"

This time, he answered truthfully. "Not really. You're still wearing clothes."

She laughed until she made it to the top of the stairs. "You were there when I lost my shit back there, weren't you?"

He nodded. "I was." Carla didn't understand that her panic attack in the alley didn't make her less attractive to him. If anything, it made her harder to resist. Even when he'd suspected that she was a mercenary brat, he'd still wanted to fuck her. But now that she'd shown some vulnerability, she was under his skin.

"I'm surprised you're not packing your shit and leaving."

The frank cuss word out of her mouth shocked him. Every second he spent with her, he felt like another layer of the façade she wore slipped away. "I don't think you're crazy."

"You're about the only one." She let out a short laugh that sounded like a honk. "Everyone in my family thinks that I've lost it."

"Because you're upset over a breakup?" That made no sense. Heartbreak was one of those things that everyone, across cultures, time, and all that shit, experienced. Her family should be understanding.

"I'm not just upset over a breakup. I'm upset over my whole life. Nothing seems right anymore. Nothing fits."

"Why?"

"I don't know." She threw up her hands. "I think I'm broken."

He walked up the stairs until he was taller than her again. She didn't step back; she looked up at him with wide eyes, filled with unshed tears. "You came here."

"Because my family didn't know what to do with me. Because I needed a place to hide."

Something in him didn't want to let her hide. He wanted to bring her out into the light again. Something about the way she was afraid of the world, someone making her afraid of the world was…tragic. He might not want anything to do with a woman who would cause him nothing but grief, but he couldn't deny his urge to prevent the sad woman standing in front of him from becoming a ghost.

He lifted his hand slowly, so she could move away from him if she wanted to. When she didn't, he trailed his index finger along her cheek, connecting her freckles. "You're still here. You're young." He had to have at least a decade on her. She was way too young for him if he was being honest. "Don't let some shit-for-brains asshole ruin your life."

"You don't even know me."

"I know enough to know that any guy who thinks you're too much for him doesn't deserve you."

"Now you're just full of shit." She shook her head, one of her red strands falling into her face. He brushed it out of the way, noting that the tears in her eyes had been replaced by irritation.

"I don't lie." It was one of the few hard-and-fast policies he applied to himself. He might omit the truth if the truth could get someone killed, but he never lied. Not after he saw what lies could do.

He pressed his thumb into the softness of her cheek, and her mouth popped open. He wanted to suck on her pink bottom lip, but he wasn't sure how she'd react. Her breath was fast and her face was pink, but she'd had a big day. He couldn't be certain that it was what she wanted.

He couldn't give her what she needed anyway.

"Go get some rest." He dropped his hand and took a step down the flight of stairs.

"I still haven't had coffee."

He turned from her and headed toward the kitchen. "I'll make some. I know where Lola has a secret stash." Coffee he could do. Emotional triage, he couldn't.

Chapter 6

Carla found a note wedged between the door and the frame when she got to her room. Turns out, Lola wasn't just gone for the day. She'd decided to go on a short trip to Santiago de Cuba in order to give Carla and Jonah some "space and privacy."

She didn't need space and privacy; she needed tender loving care from her family. What she definitely didn't need was to be stuck in Cuba with a guy—who, granted, had rescued her from sitting in an alley today and giving up—she didn't even really like.

She'd figured out what bothered her so much about him when he'd said, "I never hurt women." She felt like he was always condescending to her. It was *almost* enough to extinguish her attraction to him. And, to be honest, it was one of the reasons that she'd been relieved when Geoff broke up with her. Her ex always treated her like she was dumb. And—although she wasn't as good at math and business as her older siblings—she wasn't stupid. She was quite smart.

He'd always looked at her like she was some kind of project. And she'd shaped herself into who he wanted her to be. And she still hadn't been enough.

Well, fuck that. Jonah might have been nice to her today, but that didn't mean she owed him anything. His kindness toward her was just basic human decency. Whatever he wanted in a woman, she was the opposite.

If he thought she was a pampered, rich girl, she'd show him exactly what that looked like.

A knock sounded through her bedroom. He didn't even ask to come in before stepping into her room and sucking all the air out with him.

He put a tiny, steaming cup on the dresser. Since he'd been nice enough to carry her home and make her coffee, she resisted the urge to ask him if he'd ever heard of a coaster. "Storm's coming."

"What the fuck are you? An old-timey pirate?"

He laughed, so her aim of annoying him was failing miserably. "No. Do I look like a pirate?"

"Kind of." He totally looked like a pirate. And not one of those effete ones with bad teeth. He looked like a pirate on the cover of a romance novel. Like a present she wanted to unwrap. She could definitely picture herself draped over his arm in something diaphanous and entirely unsuitable for the time period.

"You into pirates?"

No wonder he was a photojournalist; he was certainly sparing with the whole words thing.

"No." She pursed her lips around the lie. Though she'd slipped earlier in the day, when she'd still be feeling ragged from the incident in the alley, she didn't want him to know how he affected her. She felt an inexplicable need to keep the upper hand in their interactions.

Jonah shrugged one huge shoulder. She imagined that such a minor movement in his body could dislodge a building from its foundations. She certainly felt moved by him despite her efforts to the contrary.

"There's actually a storm coming. A tropical storm that could turn into a hurricane." Jonah paused and pushed her coffee toward her, like he hadn't just announced that they could die in the next couple of days. "It wasn't supposed to hit Cuba, but it changed course last night."

"How did you find out? The Internet's for shit down here."

"Charlie called me on my satellite phone to ask me if I wanted to get on his private jet with him."

"And you didn't take him up on it?"

He just grunted and lifted a shoulder again. He was definitely staying because of Lola. If he was worried enough about Lola not to leave the island, this must be really bad.

Panic seized her immature thoughts about needling Jonah and threw them to the wayside. She could give him shit later, if they were even alive to deal with it.

"We have to find Lola."

"She'll come home soon enough. I'm sure she's just out somewhere getting supplies."

So maybe he hadn't been worried about Lola. Maybe he was worried about her. She pushed that thought away, too.

"No!" Carla couldn't keep the yell down. To think she'd been resenting her great aunt for leaving her here with Jonah when Lola could be off somewhere in danger. "She went to Santiago. For a vacation! In a hurricane!"

"Fuck." Jonah's face creased into a tableau of worry, which she could tell was genuine.

"She doesn't have a cell phone."

"Wouldn't work down here if she did." Carla had heard there were improvements in infrastructure happening, but those hadn't born themselves out in improved cell service to the island in the past few years. Still, she looked to Jonah for a likely impossible solution. "She's smart, though. She'll know to find shelter."

His words belied the same worry that Carla felt. On top of that, guilt crept in. If Carla hadn't been so limp and despondent over her stupid breakup, Lola wouldn't have felt the need to cheer her up. She wouldn't have left her here with a designated rebound guy—Jonah. And she wouldn't be in mortal peril right now.

Carla looked down at the sheet of paper; just a few words, but words that damned her. She was always causing her family grief, and this was just the worst example yet. She thought about telling her father that his favorite aunt, a woman who had survived six decades of communism, some of them quite austere, and a woman who had spied for the United States and not gotten caught or killed by the regime, was going to drown because Carla had a sad about a loser accountant breaking up with her.

Her breaths got shallow again, and she sank onto the edge of the bed. She wrapped her arms around her own waist and bent over in half, trying to get a grip. There had to be a way to save Lola.

"Why did she leave?" She didn't want to answer. One good way to make Jonah hate her would be to tell him that it was her fault that his benefactor likely wouldn't survive the next few days. And she didn't want Jonah to hate her.

"She wanted to give us 'space and privacy.'"

To her shock, he didn't recoil and call her out. He laughed and knelt down at her feet. She let him pry the note from her hand as though he needed proof of Lola's preposterous plan. Once he read the terse words, he simply said, "Fuck."

"That seems to be a recurring theme."

He put the note down next to her on the bed. Then he cupped her knees with his hands. Her breath caught, and her skin heated, burning through some of her distress. "She's going to be okay."

"How do you know that?" Tears stung the back of Carla's eyes. "This is all my fault."

"That's just fucking crazy."

"I thought we established that I'm not crazy." Given the fact that she was about to have her second panic attack, she was sensitive about people calling her crazy right now.

"I'm not saying that you are." *Despite counterevidence*, she filled in for him in the pause that followed. "I'm saying that blaming yourself for another person's actions sounds crazy."

That was better, but she knew she didn't exactly sound sane. She couldn't suppress the need to explain herself. "If I wasn't so broken up about my ex, she wouldn't have thought I needed to rebound, and she wouldn't have tried to push us together like this." She gestured toward him, and his hands tightened on her knees. Being this close to him was going to make her actually crazy if she wasn't careful. "She would be safe and sound at home instead of on the roads somewhere. She'll probably die in a mudslide, and it will be all my fault."

"She's headed to Santiago, right?" His careful tone walked the line between reassuring and condescending. She nodded. "The storm isn't tracking over that part of the island. So, we're in more danger here than she is traveling."

Oddly, the idea of being in mortal danger herself was more comforting than the nightmare of her aunt being hurt. "You're sure?"

"You can't ever be sure with the weather, but I called a meteorologist I know in New York, who gave me details."

"A *girl* meteorologist, right?" Carla scrunched up her nose at the idea of Jonah railing some ditzy weather girl.

One end of Jonah's mouth quirked up. "Jealous?"

She shook her head. "No. I'm just concerned that she might not have any incentive to give you accurate information. She might want you dead." Carla turned up her nose. "Depending on how you ended things."

Jonah leaned toward her. His face came so close to hers that his smell enveloped her. Her heart raced, and increasingly familiar heat spread through her lower belly. His half-smile was deadly. Her self-control— shaky at the best of times—was crumbling. If he stayed close to her for too much longer, it would snap like an old rubber band stored next to a hot oven. She should be able to withstand him, but she was currently in a state. Everything about her life was in flux, and she couldn't be expected to *not* kiss him at this point.

Her eyelids drifted to half-mast, and she leaned in until their lips were almost touching.

"Believe me, princess." His lips barely brushed hers as he growled at her. "No one I've ever been with wants me dead. They want more."

"Cocky." She knew that word sounded like less of an insult and more of a breathy tease, but she couldn't help it. He was intoxicating, and she was helpless against the power of her own lust. Lust that had swept away her anxiety of Lola's safety in a split second.

He was going to close the distance between their mouths. He *had* to. But the longer he stayed still the more she worried that he was going to make her pull the trigger. She'd never made the first move because she'd never had to. This was entirely new territory. Both feeling like she did for him and wanting to take control were new.

Hell, maybe Lola was right, and she needed to get under Jonah to get over getting dumped. She stretched up just slightly and sealed their mouths together. Still, he didn't take the lead like she'd expected him to. Instead, he held still, his hands on her knees as she brushed against his lips with hers. She ran her teeth against his criminally soft lower lip.

He made a *huff* sound, but he still didn't move. Maybe he didn't want to kiss her at all. Maybe he was letting her kiss him so she wouldn't fall apart again. The last thing he needed was her balled up in a corner in the middle of a natural disaster. Perhaps he was just humoring her for a few seconds?

She started to pull away, disappointed and embarrassed. But he tightened his grip on her thighs and ran his hands up, up, and nearly to her panties. Her body convulsed against the sudden stimulation. She opened her eyes and found him staring at her.

"Okay?"

His thumbs were pressed into her skin just right, which seemed to have a direct dial connection to her clit. *Okay?* This was so much more than *okay*, and he hadn't even kissed her back.

She didn't answer; she just went back in for another kiss. This time, he gave her what she'd wanted the first time. He took over—teasing and taunting. There were teeth and tongues, and she melted against his hardness. She reached up and buried her fingers in his hair, pulling it until his mouth opened and the kiss went deeper. It was like the first few minutes that they'd met. That touch of hatred that made the chemistry between them so much hotter.

She'd never had hate sex before, but she'd never really hated anyone on sight either. She couldn't explain how their alchemy worked if someone asked, but she didn't care. All she knew was that she had to have him. If his kiss was this satisfying, then fucking him would probably kill her.

And that's how she wanted to die, not gasping for air in a dirty alley, paralyzed by her own panic.

* * * *

Carla was sweeter than he'd ever imagined. Her petal-pink mouth had driven him crazy from the moment they met. The only reason he hadn't laid her out the second she pressed that sweetness to his mouth was shock. He'd been pretty sure that his desire for her was one-sided. He'd tried to be careful, making sure it was okay to touch her during her panic attack. He was so sure that contact with him wasn't something she wanted that he wasn't able to compute when *she'd touched him.*

His scalp stung where her long, manicured nails dug in and pulled against his hair, as though she was steering him around her mouth. Fuck that. If she was going to spring a kiss on him, knocking him off his game, he was going to have some fun.

When he moved one hand off her thigh, gripping the back of her head, she let out a frustrated moan. When he stopped kissing her mouth, angled her head back, and ran his tongue up the cord of her throat, she stopped breathing.

He'd come in here to warn her about the storm and to start making plans to secure the house, but one kiss and he couldn't care less if the whole thing crumbled into a pile around them. He had to get inside her. No longer caring that she was trouble, he maneuvered both of them so that she was flat on her back on the bed, and he held himself over her. He'd thought she was soft and fragile, especially after this morning, until she'd taken it upon herself to kiss him and then pull his hair.

But that might have been her coming down off the adrenaline high of a panic attack. He didn't know her well enough to guess.

He'd gone along with the kiss and taken it further because she had tapped into something elemental about him. Something that had led him to carry her home like a caveman and press her into the mattress as though he intended to fuck her until the storm ended instead of just keeping her safe. His cock was doing all the thinking because it was so full that he was going to come all over her pretty soft skin if he didn't slow this down.

He pulled back. Carla's skin was flushed, and her chest heaved like she'd just run a marathon. "Do you want this?"

She shocked him again by pinching his side. "Would I be doing it otherwise?"

"Ow."

"Don't be a baby." She pushed at him until he sat down next to her. Then, she got up off the bed. "I was kissing you because I wanted to. I might be having some issues right now because I've been thrown a curveball, but I'm not stupid or reckless or anything like that. I'm stronger than I look."

Jonah was getting that impression the more time he spent with her. "I don't think that."

"Yes, you do. Why else would you not have kissed me back until I practically forced you? You're going to make me feel like a real creep."

She had him there. Truth was, he was always careful when it came to sex. He didn't want there to be any miscommunication. And he never wanted anyone to feel like he had taken advantage of them. He'd always been proactive about making people comfortable around him. His sheer size scared some people off, so he always tried to make it clear that he wasn't a threat. Although some people would always see him that way because he trusted the wrong person once.

"You just had a big morning, and I wasn't sure what you were trying to do." He was getting the impression that she was, in fact, stronger than she looked. She was a lot more than she put forward when she showed up at the door. Seeing her vulnerable like this morning and angry like now made him realize that he might have been too quick to judge her. One corner of her mouth kicked up. "Do you want to try again?"

"We should probably be battening down hatches, or some such, don't you think?"

Oh, yeah. He'd almost let himself forget about that. "You have your coffee to drink."

She walked over to the dresser and picked up the cup. Given how intent she'd been on getting coffee this morning—so much so that she'd risked leaving the house—he expected her to chug it. Instead, she took a dainty sip and sighed with pleasure. Everything below his waist tightened when she parted her lips. It made him think of her parting them for his cock. It made him want to see how she would sigh when he sank into her.

Maybe he was the crazy one, thinking about all the ways he'd like to fuck her after one kiss. One kiss that she probably regretted about now.

He forced himself to stop looking at her.

"Thank you."

"For what?" He wanted to know if she was more grateful for the ride home in his arms, the coffee, or the kiss.

"Everything." One word gave him hope that he might get more of the kissing. After all, they'd be stuck together for a couple of days at least.

Chapter 7

Holy fuck, could Carla Hernandez organize shit. He wasn't sure how she'd done it, but within a matter of hours, she'd inventoried all their supplies, found a way to get more of what they'd needed, and had sorted out a couple of Lola's elderly neighbors.

All Jonah had done was hammer some boards and fill some sandbags, following her directions.

Just in time, too. The winds had picked up, and the sky had gone gray and sickly green in places. She needed to get back to the house—and soon. Carla was at one last neighbor's place, making sure she had enough food and some boiled water to get through a power outage.

He should have gone with her. The way he'd started to feel responsible for her right after meeting her should freak him out. Every second that she wasn't in his sight made Jonah more anxious. After seeing her get Lola's house ready for the storm, he was sure that this morning's anxiety attack had been an anomaly. No wonder she'd been upset with him seeing her like that. Something about her competence this morning had made him think that this was who she really was.

But knowing she could take care of her own shit—and everyone else's—didn't make him any less worried about her out in the building storm. She was so small she could blow away or get swept up in a flash flood as soon as it started raining.

His friend had said that they could expect thirty-nine inches. Jonah hadn't missed his former paramour's out-of-place double entendre when she'd said it. The joke had missed. His dick was big, but it wasn't that big.

It started raining, fat drops that would soak Carla through in an instant if she was out in it. He was just as worried about himself for fretting like a nursemaid as he was about Carla getting home safe. But he'd seen a flash flood getting out of control before. He knew people who had died in natural disasters. This kind of shit where everyone said that everything was going to be okay made him nervous.

Just when he was ready to go out in the storm and fetch Carla by hand, she burst through the front door. Her filmy little top and shorts were soaked through, and he wasn't that worried about her being cold; he was worried about how fast he could get her out of those wet clothes and on her back.

His mind went blank because he could see pert nipples poking at her top. He couldn't make out the lines of a bra. She must not be wearing one. Like usual. Thinking about her tits hanging free had his mouth filling with saliva. The need to taste her almost had him walking across the foyer and carrying her caveman-style up the stairs to fuck her until the storm passed. That way, neither of them would have the time to worry about flooding or the speed of the wind.

Instead, he said, "You're wet."

"You're obvious." She squeezed a puddle of water out of her hair and onto the marble foyer floor. "Did you get all the windows boarded?"

He nodded. "We're all safe and snug in here." But he really wasn't sure. They were protected by a sea wall, but who knew when that would crumble. If the tide breached the barrier, the roads would be a washout, and Lola's house could get flooded to the second floor. Worst-case scenario, they ended up stuck on the roof. That wasn't really the worst-case scenario, but he was trying not to think of anything beyond that.

"Did you take the nonperishables to the second floor?"

"I did everything you told me to."

"Good boy." Her words were laced with sarcasm, but she didn't quite pull it off because she was shivering. He wanted to get her naked and warm her up, but he needed to step back for a hot minute. He wasn't thinking clearly around this woman, and that could get him into trouble if he wasn't extremely careful. If anything was going to happen between them, it needed to unfold slowly.

"Don't talk to me like I'm your lap dog."

"Oh, I know you're not."

Looking at her there, soaked through and succulent, terrified him. Like something in him knew that she wasn't just demanding on a surface level. She would take everything he had to give her and more, just because she could. She might seem dainty and sweet, but she was the most dangerous kind of woman there was. She was a wolf in sheep's clothing.

She looked right back at him, a wry grin passing across her mouth, as though she knew what kind of power she had over men. As though she reveled in it.

"Can I ask you something?"

"What do you want to know?" She pinched a bit of the fabric of her top, flapping it in between her fingers. In the hall light, the movement revealed a silhouette of the underside of her breast. He bit his lip, knowing that she would see what he wanted to do to that fleshy bit right then.

"Why are you so calm getting ready for the storm?" As a follow-up, he wanted to know if she liked fucking doggy-style or up against a wall. He'd give her both if she asked, but he *needed* to know what she wanted more right now.

"You mean how am I so calm now when I was a basket case earlier?" His face heated. Although he had only meant to distract himself from wanting to fuck Carla through a mattress, he'd poked at something that clearly bothered her and embarrassed her. She was probably going to toss him out in the storm now. "I guess, but I don't think you were a basket case."

"Well, I do." She walked closer to him, her damp heat permeating his skin. "I got dumped. A gajillion people get dumped every day. And now I can't even take a little street harassment? I'm wandering the streets like a lost, little moppet for no good reason. If it wasn't happening to me, I wouldn't believe it."

"You were going to marry this guy?" Jonah hated this guy. Not only was he a loser, he was a loser who'd gotten to see Carla naked. A muscle in her cheek ticked as she nodded. "If you were going to marry him, he probably meant a lot to you."

"Everything." And now Jonah hated this dude even more. From what he saw today, Carla threw everything into a situation if it truly mattered to her. If she had given a guy everything, then he'd better have done everything he could to deserve her.

"Well, he's an idiot. So now you're freaked out because you gave everything to an idiot."

She threw her head back and sighed. "It's so embarrassing. All my friends are married, and most of them are expecting their first baby. And I get left at the altar. It's all anyone could talk about when I would show up someplace for months. Eventually, I just stopped going."

"It sounds like your friends have boring lives." He knew he shouldn't talk about something without properly chewing on the words first. He knew he could come off as judgmental sometimes.

"That's judgmental. You don't know their lives." Her face was pink again, and when he looked down at her arms, the goose bumps she'd had when she walked through the door disappeared.

"I know they don't have anything more interesting to do than talk shit about your life." He shrugged, and her gaze dropped to his chest. "So, I'm guessing their lives are extremely boring."

"You probably think you're better than everyone else because you travel the world snapping pictures." Her cheeks weren't just pink now; they were red, and she looked like she was about to hurl her purse at him. "What do you have to show for it? A family? No, you had to glom on to mine and accuse Lola's real family of trying to bilk her. You're a pompous asshole."

She tried to slip by him, but he grabbed her arm, surprising himself. He let go the instant she looked down on his hand with disdain.

* * * *

They'd been doing so well.

He hadn't sniped at her once or even called her "princess" in a tone that bothered her in several hours. And she'd been feeling good about what she'd gotten done that day. She was always better when she had a project to work on. Who knew that storm preparation had a lot in common with party planning?

And then he had to go and be an asshole about her friends. Well, fuck that. She tried to stomp into the kitchen, but it was lame, with her sopping wet and wearing no shoes. She should head up to the bathroom to dry off, but she saw the way he looked at her while she was trying to get some of the damp out of her top. It was the same way he'd looked at her earlier. In her bedroom. Right before he'd kissed her back.

Even though he pretty much sucked, she liked having him look at her that way. And, since they were stuck here for the next twenty-four hours or so, she was going to make him look, but not touch, all night long.

She peeked into the refrigerator and got herself a cold beer. Since the power would likely go out, she would enjoy it while she could. The rum could wait for later. Alcohol would maybe help with the wanting-to kill-her-erstwhile-roommate situation.

She rested her head against the outdated stone countertop, exhausted to her bones. It wasn't bad, necessarily. But she hadn't felt this way in months. Staying inside had killed her business, which was another reason for her coming down here. Her father was going to pay her to redecorate the house. It wouldn't make her even with her parents, not even close. They'd laid out almost a hundred thousand dollars for her wedding, and a lot of that had been forfeited when they'd canceled. So, her breakup was more than an embarrassment, it was just another reason for her to believe she didn't measure up to the family standard.

Jonah came into the kitchen with a towel. "Dry off."

He was so imperious, and it made her hot. She was still bent over at the waist, and she wanted to arch her back even more when he gave her that order.

His gaze dipped to her ass, which made her stand up even more slowly. She wondered what it would feel like if he smacked it. Would both cheeks fit in one of his palms? Probably not, but the power he could put into a spanking would probably press her pelvic bone against the edge of the counter. She could probably come that way. And she wanted to test that hypothesis right now despite the fact that Jonah was an asshole who thought she was frivolous and silly.

But, every time she got a smell or an eyeful of him, she couldn't seem to care. She stood up and looked her fill. Took a deep gulp of beer.

"Little early for that, don't you think?"

"I figure that lots of beer is the only way to make being stuck here with you any fun at all."

"You know what won't be fun?" He shook the towel at her, which made her want to take it even less. "Walking pneumonia."

When she didn't take the towel from his hand, he unfolded it and wrapped it around her.

"You sound like my mother."

"At least I don't look like her."

She knew he probably didn't mean it to sound like her mother was unfortunate-looking, but she wasn't about to let it pass. "I do, so what's wrong with the way I look?"

He stilled for a moment. "Nothing."

Carla craned her neck and looked up at him. He hadn't backed away when giving her the towel, and she pressed herself closer, mindless of the fact that she'd probably get him all wet.

"You hated me on sight, so there has to be something." She sure as hell felt something now. The bulge in his jeans was proportional to everything out of his jeans. He might think she was empty-headed, but his cock didn't give a crap.

He put his hands on her shoulders like he was going to push her away. Instead, he lifted her up by the waist and sat her on the counter. She still wasn't at his eye level, so he leaned in close and gave his crafty villain smile. "Now, you've got me all wet."

"Will you take your pants off?" She took another sip of beer. "I'd hate for that jumbo-sized treat in your pants to shrivel up."

"No chance of that happening with you around."

A tingling started in her chest. She was shocked that he'd admitted that he was to attracted her. Especially since she wasn't ready to admit that they had chemistry out loud. She was still at the teasing and innuendo part of their situation. He was going to steal her fun if he took the bait too soon. But, then again, she'd probably give up the game entirely for some of what he could dish out.

"You don't hate me then?"

"I never hated you." He grabbed the towel again and rubbed her head with it. Being handled like she was a child coming out of her bath shouldn't turn her on as much as it did. "I just didn't trust you. I don't really trust anyone."

"Do you trust me now?"

He didn't answer, and her stomach swirled with unease. She didn't know why it was important that he trust her, just that it was important. After all, they were kind of a team in getting through this storm.

"Kind of." He dropped the towel to the counter. "But that's about as good as it gets for me."

"I'll take it." *For now.*

"You did good getting us sorted for the storm. I've seen professionals start panicking when they realize that they're actually going to have to weather a natural disaster in a place that's ill equipped to handle it. You didn't panic."

Carla beamed under his praise but tried not to show it outwardly. She looked down. "I don't know. I just don't think there's any use in panicking." She didn't miss the irony, remembering herself in the alley. "When there's actually something to worry about."

She gulped the rest of her beer so that she wouldn't grab onto Jonah and try for another kiss. It would really help if he moved away, but he didn't seem to be in any rush to do that.

"Any more of those beers in the fridge?" He still didn't move away.

"Plenty." She gestured. "You should get one. They'll skunk if the power goes out."

That earned her a smile and butterflies all over her body, but he still didn't go get this beer he seemed so interested in talking about. "Wouldn't have guessed that you liked beer."

"Why not?" Her voice sounded husky and desirous, and she couldn't help it. She licked her lips.

"Princesses usually don't."

"I'm not as much of a princess as you think I am."

He dipped his head and nuzzled into her hair. Her breath caught. She had been expecting him to kiss her—wanting and waiting for it—but she hadn't expected him to waste time doing something as silly as smelling her hair. He was probably getting a nose full of acid rain, but she hardly cared. The heat of him so close to her skin caused something inside her to bloom, soften, open up to anything he wanted to give her.

"You smell like rain."

"Is that good?" *Please let it be good. She wanted him to want her.*

His only answer was an, "Mmmm," as he moved her hair away from her neck and put his lips on her skin, tasting her flesh. She'd never felt so savored before, and it made her restless for more.

"What are you doing to me?"

The question made him stop, which was the last thing he wanted to happen. "Do you not want this? Weren't you just sticking those tight little cheeks up in the air, hoping to drive me crazy so I would touch you here." He palmed her in between her legs, punctuating his thought, and driving her mad.

She moved her legs further apart. How could she want him so much when he was in such control? He went back to kissing her neck, but he didn't move his hand. Without volition, she pressed herself against him, praying for the fabric to move so she could feel his fingers against her skin. She wanted to jump inside him.

He moved down to her collarbone, his touches still maddeningly soft against her skin. She made a sound of protest, and he lifted his head again. "What's wrong?"

"I want more."

He braced his hands around her hips, leaving her wanting—again. "You want more?"

She nodded. With his hands off of her, she noticed how uncomfortable her damp clothes were against her skin, a slight musty smell starting to grow.

"If I give you more, you might not want it." She didn't miss the grimace on his face.

"You're worried your dick is too big?" If he thought her eyes were bigger than her vagina, he had another think coming. When she'd thought about him the night before, he was just as big as what she'd felt in his pants. She had to remedy him of the erroneous idea that she was a delicate flower right about now. "I assure you that I am fully prepared to take whatever you give me."

To make her point clear, she snaked her hand in between them and cupped him. He dropped his head back and made an animal noise, but he didn't back off. He never backed off completely, but he seemed shy about sealing the deal. Her teasing him when he first came into the kitchen must have confused him. Or maybe he thought she was the one who was confused about what she wanted.

They were totally wrong for each other in a myriad of ways. She liked to stay close to her family in Miami; she wanted to see them more than once or twice a year. He traveled the world, most of the time looking for trouble—big trouble like war and famine. He thought she was silly and frivolous. She thought he was a judgmental jerk. She wanted a husband and babies. He wanted the next adventure.

This would be extremely time-limited, just for as long as they were trapped by the storm, but she needed what he had to offer. As hard and as often as he had to give it to her.

"You think you're going to hurt me?"

"I know I am." He pressed a hand to his abdomen, which she followed with hers, lifting his shirt. If he didn't take it off, she was going to start feeling like a creep. She didn't care as soon as her fingers met his smooth, ridged skin. He must live in a gym when he wasn't on the road. "I'm so big, and you're tiny."

"You can't possibly be as obtuse about how human coitus works as you sound right about now." She wiggled her fingers into the waistband of his jeans. His pants were loose, so her fingers found the base of his cock. "You'll fit."

He grunted and pushed his hips toward her. "I know." The knowledge that she could make him lose control sent chills all over her body, unrelated to the fact that she was wearing wet clothes. But his eyes snapped open.

"You're cold."

"No, I'm not."

"Don't argue with me."

"Why not?"

"Because it makes me want to do things to you?"

"Really, like what?"

"I want to tear those little shorts off." He ran his fingers under the hem. "And I want to turn you over and spank you."

No one had ever spanked Carla before, no matter how bad or good she'd been. Her pussy went wet and soft as her fantasy came to life with his words. "Go on."

"You really need me to fill in the blanks?" She scored through the hair surrounding his cock with her nails. "Fuck. Your hand is practically wrapped around my dick, and you want me to give you a play-by-play of the ways I'm going to fuck you if you let me."

"Yes. It turns me on to hear you say it." She pulled her hand out of his pants, pulled his shirt up, and ran her tongue along the line between the muscles of his abdomen. "What happens after you spank me?"

"I'm going to want to see how red I made those cheeks."

Carla got his shirt up over his nipples and took a bite of one. His groan shook his chest. It shook her. She wanted to squeeze her legs together, maybe get his hand back there. She needed relief. "Why?"

"Why do I want to spank you?" He got his act together and pushed his hand down the back of her shorts, squeezing her flesh there. "Because watching you walk up a staircase is a religious experience."

No one had ever said that about her ass before. She'd always thought it was disproportionally big for the rest of her body. But his hot hand against her chilled flesh made her want them both naked now.

"You want to spank me now?" She pulled his shirt over his head and took a minute to admire his torso. She'd been so taken with the muscles in his legs a few days ago, she hadn't had the opportunity to pay homage to the rest of his truly spectacular physique. "Dude, how much do you work out?"

Then, he blushed. And it shocked the shit out of her and made her curious about him. He was this perfectly gorgeous man who seemed ashamed of several of the things that made him appealing. If he didn't want people appreciating his body, he shouldn't walk around looking like a damn superhero.

"It keeps my mind busy."

She supposed that his job was stressful, and it might be good for him to blow off steam, especially if he was in a conflict zone. She had to think about mimosas in order to get through a spinning class. And that seemed shallow next to the things that Jonah likely experienced frequently. But this was about sexy times, not her own damage. "What else do you do to keep busy?"

He ran his hands up her lower back, taking her top with them. "I'm glad you're not wearing one of those stupid little romper things again."

She didn't miss that he didn't answer her question, but maybe the answer was sex. And, even though this was temporary, she didn't want to think about him doing this with anyone else. Especially spanking. Spanking was *her* thing now. If only she could get him to do it and seal the deal. "Rompers aren't stupid."

"They are stupid because they make it harder for me to get you naked."

"Nuh-uh. They are only one piece. One piece is easier than two pieces."

He pulled her top off instead of continuing the argument. They'd only known each other for a few days, but she was beginning to understand how he interacted with others. If she asked a question he didn't like, he didn't answer it. He said something else or did something to piss her off. Now he had her taking off her shirt because she was no longer thinking about her wardrobe and relative ease of removing items, she was looking at him, looking at her with something on his face that approached awe.

She liked it, but it kicked up her heart rate. "Are you just going to stand there looking at them?"

"No. But I want to remember these."

"So you can jack off to them later." She leaned back. "I mean I guess I'm flattered, but I'd rather you try to remember them with your mouth."

He swooped in and took one of her nipples between his teeth. She jumped but grabbed his head to keep him there. He pulled more of her breast in his mouth and licked her slowly and just the right way. Her mouth dropped open, and whatever he was doing to her traveled straight to her clit.

More than his mouth got down to business. He pulled down her shorts and panties and somehow lifted her up and pulled them off without her doing anything to help.

"Your size makes it possible for you to do that." She dropped her head back when his lips traveled down her belly, and he held her open with his hands. "I like how big you are."

He hadn't even made her come yet, and she wanted to tie him up and bring him back to Miami with her. She could resume her previous social schedule and endure the pitying looks and outright scorn from the other Junior Leaguers if she was getting it every night from this guy.

When his mouth found her center she melted into him. She raised her head and looked down, wanting to commit this to memory so she could refer to him inside her as her very own form of anxiety relief.

"It's so good." She knew she sounded surprised, but it had been so long. Geoff had gone down on her every once in a while, but he'd never had what she would call an "assertive tongue." He'd gamely hung out down there, but she'd had to do all the work, oftentimes to no avail.

This was so much better because Jonah held her hips still while he took his time tasting her. He used the perfect pressure, but he didn't get into a groove, no repeats. Everything he did felt awesome, but her orgasm couldn't get a head of steam behind it.

"Please." She hated having to beg for anything, but begging for an orgasm was just pathetic. Unless it was the one that Jonah owed her after all this time between her legs. "Stop fucking around."

He lifted his head, and she had to bite the inside of her cheek to keep from yelling in frustration.

"You are so used to getting what you want, aren't you, princess?

"You don't know anything about me." Truth told, she hadn't had an orgasm by anything but her own hand in ages. But she wasn't about to tell him that truth. He'd feel sorry for her. She didn't want a pity orgasm from him. She wanted the real deal. She wanted it because he wanted to be down there. "But when a man has his mouth between my legs, I expect to come."

He sat back on his heels, bracing his hands on his upper legs. He was still almost eye level with all of her good bits. "I was getting to that part." He shook his head with a wicked smile. "You really do have to learn to enjoy the journey more, princess."

"Stop calling me that. I'm at enough risk of losing my lady boner as it is." He stood up on his knees and grabbed her legs again, as if he thought he could assuage her with touch. He could. "I just happen to really like this particular destination, and I'd be much obliged if you take the direct route to getting there."

"And that would be?"

He was asking her? She felt sort of ridiculous explaining exactly what she wanted him to do, but his thumbs were rubbing the crease between her thighs and her pussy. It made her pathetic situation desperate. "Just do the sucking thing. The licking thing is nice, but it's a diversion."

Before she'd gotten all the words out, he swooped in and started with the sucking thing. After the pause, it was almost too intense. She wasn't about to complain because it went from too much to just enough very quickly. Her muscles twitched, and she grabbed at his hair. When he added a tongue swoop, it pulled her over the edge, and she came. She whimpered and slumped over his head, effectively trapping him.

Chapter 8

Holy shit. Touching and kissing with Carla was more intense than any sexual encounter Jonah could remember. He wasn't sure if it was the fact that she kind of hated him that did it for him or what.

The X factor that had him reeling from touching her kept him close to her. She was probably wanting to move soon. Right about now, she would decide that she was done with him.

She surprised him by wrapping her arms around his head and hugging him. "That was amazing."

"It was."

She giggled, and the sound filled him with lust and warmth in his chest. "It was amazing for you? I nearly crushed your thick head."

That had him laughing. He stood up, grabbing the towel, and wrapping it around her. He examined her face for any hint of regret. He wouldn't be able to stand it if she regretted what they'd just done.

He wiped off his mouth and beard with the back of his hand.

Her green eyes were clear, and the light danced off her face in a way that had him wanting to grab his camera.

Instead, he cupped her face in his hands and kissed her. She stiffened in shock at first, and so he stilled. He hoped she didn't find kissing him after where his mouth had been offensive. She didn't pull away; she wrapped her arms around him and kissed him back, losing the towel in the process.

Her desire for him knocked him off center, and he realized why he'd been so hostile to her the day they'd met. She terrified him. If she wanted, she could have him at her beck and call, no begging required.

And that thought didn't make him pull away. It made him savor her taste, the feel of all her naked flesh pressed against his torso, the fluttering and grabbing of her delicate but strong hands as she touched him everywhere.

His erection pressed against the fly of his jeans, demanding relief. But, where he couldn't deny Carla her pleasure, he was determined to deny himself. If he fucked her, this became more than a way to assuage boredom, they would be involved. She might get emotional about him and inevitably be disappointed in him when he couldn't give her everything she needed.

Because he would always leave. That's the way he'd set up his life, and that suited him. He wasn't about to quit traveling and buy a condo in Miami so he could set up house with a woman who was used to having everything. He simply didn't have enough to offer her.

So he pulled away. "You should get some clothes on."

She tilted her head to the side and she looked at his cock, which had apparently decided to punch at his belt until he ached even more to be inside her. "But what about—"

"We have all night." If he made it sound like he was going to fuck her eventually, maybe it wouldn't be a big deal when it didn't happen. They could do other stuff. He could make sure she came a bunch more times. "We should get hot showers while that's still an option."

She pulled the towel back over her shoulders and nodded. "I'll put some food together. We should eat some of the stuff that will go bad if the power goes out."

She was running upstairs with her ass hanging out of the towel when he remembered that he'd meant to spank her.

* * * *

Was there such a thing as placating someone with cunnilingus? Carla couldn't get that question and a million others about what had happened in the kitchen out of her head while she showered.

Her body still thrummed with what he had done to her, and she was thinking about how much more she wanted. For starters, she wanted to see what he was hiding in his pants. She'd felt enough to know that his worries about being too big were not *completely* ridiculous. She just didn't care. Just like some people couldn't stop themselves from climbing Mount Everest, nothing was going to stop her from returning Jonah's little favor.

Her skin was still reddened from his beard and her lips still felt swollen from his kisses. She'd probably looked sex-crazed downstairs, and at this point, she was beyond caring.

She'd convince him to fuck her tonight no matter what the cost— begging, cajoling, seducing, sitting in his lap and grinding until he lost all control—she'd pay it. She wasn't proud anymore.

The way he'd backed off from her when she'd suggested they fuck made her think that he didn't really want her. Maybe it had been pity cunnilingus? Placating pity cunnilingus.

She didn't know if that was more or less pathetic than being left on the altar. At least no one back home would find out that she wasn't even capable of closing the deal on a one-night stand anymore. If she failed in her mission, she wouldn't even tell her sister.

No, her blissfully happy, *engaged* sister would never let her hear the end of it. In a month, Alana was marrying her one and only one-night stand. Standing on the altar next to her older sister was going to gut her, but she had to do it. That had been part of what coming down here was about. Her father had thought—and she'd eventually agreed—that she needed to get away from her familiar surroundings and make herself useful if she was going to get past the issues that had cropped up when Geoff dumped her.

After a day of getting people organized and helping people prepare for the storm, she'd felt invigorated. And after getting turned out on the kitchen counter, she was more determined than ever to get her life back.

Part of her wanted to explain to Jonah why she needed him, just for tonight, just until the storm passed. But would he really want to know that she was using him to rebound from a relationship that hadn't been all that great to begin with?

Sparring with Jonah, as annoying as it was when he called her "princess," was more exciting than most of the conversations that she and Geoff had had in their entire relationship. She'd always felt as though she was managing him, and it had been exhausting.

She was starting to think she hadn't even liked Geoff all that much. The longer they were together, the less she was of herself. He didn't like going to parties, so she'd stopped planning them. He didn't like fancy restaurants—he said they were too expensive—so she'd learned to cook. He didn't want to fork out for a cleaning service, even though she'd offered to pay for it, so she'd spent afternoon upon afternoon scrubbing floors and polishing countertops.

And he hadn't even thanked her. He'd never brought her flowers. He was just there, until he wasn't.

Before she knew it, she'd become depressed. She'd lost touch with friends and caused problems with her family. She'd been so jealous when her sister found Cole and started having hot sex, she'd told their brother—Cole's best friend. The drama had almost broken Cole and Alana up.

She'd also made the wrong first impression with Javi's now-fiancée, Maya. Maya was the coolest girl in the world, and Carla had acted like a total snob when she'd showed up.

Her family had forgiven her, but they always did. They didn't hold her accountable for shitty behavior because they expected it from her. And that hurt. She was not the woman that she wanted to be, and she needed to take steps toward changing that. She needed to reconnect with her friends and earn her family's respect.

The water had turned cold while she stood in the shower, moping about being a fuckup. She certainly wouldn't be earning Jonah's respect when he got into a cold shower. Once she got downstairs, she'd have to make him a dope dinner.

And maybe give him another way to warm up.

* * * *

Jonah knocked on the bathroom door when Carla had been in the shower for twenty minutes. A lot of shit had gone down today, and maybe she'd passed out. He hadn't seen her eat anything, and she'd had a beer. One beer on an empty stomach in someone that small could be trouble.

Fuck. What if she hadn't wanted to do what they'd done in the kitchen, and she was hiding from him? Knocking on the door wasn't going to make her any less afraid of him.

He was about to turn away when the shower turned off. So, she was still conscious. He knocked again before he could stop himself. "Are you okay?"

He expected her to shout, "Go away! You're a jerk." Instead, she opened the door, and all the blood in his brain that had been spinning tales about how he was the worst guy and how she probably couldn't stand him went to his dick. Her hair was all pushed back off her shoulders, and her skin looked so soft he wanted to sink into it for hours.

"I'm fine." She cocked her head, and a smile spread slowly across her achingly gorgeous face. "Were you worried about me? I can assure you that I've been showering by myself without incident since I was five or six."

"You had a beer—" He knew he sounded silly, but he didn't want there to be any question that she'd consented to what happened in the kitchen.

"You think I let you eat me out because I was drunk?" Her head fell forward, and her shoulders shook; he hoped she might drop the towel because he was a total pervert. "I had a panic attack. I'm not an invalid or a twelve-year-old girl, even though I look like one in the chestal area."

Her boobs were perfect, but this wasn't the time to tell her that. "I just hadn't seen you eat today."

"I totally snacked. You must not have been watching me carefully enough." He hadn't been able to keep his eyes off her. He wasn't going to tell her that either because he was aware it made him sound like a stalker.

"Oh."

"And I'm Irish and Cuban. If I can't drink one beer without jumping on any dick that happens to float by, my family would renounce me."

"I'm just a floating appendage?"

"No. I happen to like the package this," she pointed at his groin, "comes attached to."

"You just like the package?"

"You're fishing for compliments, so I'm not going to answer that." To his grave disappointment, she tightened the towel around her instead of dropping it and showing her appreciation for his package. "I am, however, going to get dressed."

Pity. Jonah clenched his fists at his sides. He wanted to fuck sassy Carla so badly that his jaw started to ache from restraining all the filthy thoughts he had about her in his mouth. And, when she deliberately squeezed his cock through his jeans as she moved past him in the doorway, his control reached its outer limit.

He was about to snap. The need to ride her sweet little body, make it sheen with sweat the same way she'd glowed from the moisture of the shower, overwhelmed him. He got undressed and into the stall that was about two sizes too small for him. Even the lukewarm spray didn't dull his need. His cock was so full it hurt. If he tried to walk right now, he'd probably be bowlegged out of courtesy to it.

But he didn't stroke it. He wanted to save that for Carla. While he was imagining how it would go down, he remembered a key fact—he hadn't brought condoms down to the island. There was no way he would fuck her without one; he didn't do that. There was plenty of other stuff they could do, but sinking into her tight wetness was the only thing he wanted. It dominated his thoughts until he rested his head against the shower wall and squeezed the tip of his cock in a vain attempt to ease his anguish.

Chapter 9

Jonah's disappointment and unease didn't relent when he walked back into the kitchen and saw Carla moving around the kitchen. She didn't look like the woman who'd been paralyzed by her own panic that morning or the competent organizer from the afternoon. Her movements were loose and easy. She hummed to herself while she seasoned something. The lights were still on, so she hadn't lit candles, but there was the same sense of cloistered softness about her right now that candles might create.

He sounded like a romantic, and that usually wasn't him. But there was something about Carla that softened the hard shell he surrounded himself with. He wasn't sure whether or not he liked it, and he was sure it wouldn't cause any permanent changes in him. This was an interlude.

There might be sex—non-penetrative unfortunately—but there wouldn't be emotion. They didn't have time for that.

"What's cooking?"

She didn't start, so she must have known he was watching her, and allowed it. "I'm just freshening up some *ropa vieja* from last night with a salad."

His stomach grumbled at the thought of food. She wasn't the only one who'd missed meals today while battening down the hatches. "Sounds amazing." He knew he sounded like a lecher when he said that. But everything around Carla turned into something sensual. At least everything for him.

She picked up two large plates of food and nodded her head towards the fridge. "Get two beers."

He obliged her, although he wasn't thirsty for beer. They ought to have a serious conversation about what could happen and what could not happen tonight. Because shit was going down. But they had to remain sensible and in control.

He waited until they sat down and had taken a few bites of food. It was delicious, like all Lola's food was, but he had a pit in his stomach. He didn't know why he was so nervous. Carla was the only woman who'd made him nervous in a dog's age.

"We can't have sex tonight."

She choked on her food, coughing until he patted her on the back once, hard. Then, she started laughing, long and uproarious. The long peals of her amusement were almost hysterical in volume, pitch, and duration. She laughed for so long he was afraid it was turning into another panic attack.

"Are you okay?"

She slowly pulled her laughter back and wiped the tears off her face. "Thank you. That was good."

"What was good?"

"That joke. The one about us not having sex tonight." She took a bite of food and stared at him while she chewed. He didn't know what she was talking about so he stayed silent. "You were joking, right? I mean, we already had sex on the kitchen counter. My great aunt's kitchen counter. We sullied the tiles, probably forever."

"I don't have protection."

"We can still do other stuff."

"But I want to get inside you."

Her lips curled into a smile so sexy it made him angry. "You do? How badly do you want to get inside me? Describe it."

"I was glad the shower was cold." He didn't have words for how he wanted her.

"Really? Did that make your hard-on go away?"

He couldn't believe she was casually asking about his erection and chewing on *ropa vieja*. He'd been all wrong about her. She wasn't uptight. She was possibly as much of a pervert as he was. "No."

"I could help you with that without a condom."

"I think you like making me uncomfortable."

Her knowing smile said he wasn't wrong. "I won't deny that I like seeing you blush. It takes my mind off worrying about Lola and whether my family in Florida is safe."

"Well, then. Embarrass away."

"I don't think you're embarrassed."

"You're wrong there."

"What do you have—we have—to be embarrassed about?"

She put more food on his plate. He liked that she was taking care of him. Aside from Lola, he didn't often have someone seeing to his needs. But, where his affection for Lola was maternal, his feelings for Carla were decidedly more primal. He wasn't a chest-beating caveman, but he wanted to claim her despite the fact that they were all wrong for each other. Her feeding him was bad—unless he wanted to make a terrible mistake tonight.

"We're just eating dinner. And the only reason we're eating together is the storm outside."

The wind had picked up yet again, and metal hit stone somewhere outside. The lights flickered but didn't go out—not yet. The limited light from the darkening sky and the boarded-up windows made the room feel more intimate somehow.

His flesh rippled with the need to clear the plates from the table with a sweep of his arm and take her right there. He wanted to show her that he wasn't embarrassed about anything he wanted to do to her. No, he was ashamed that he couldn't control his reactions to her. He was angry at himself for his thinking about her the day they'd met. When she'd knocked on the door, he'd dismissed her as an annoyance, and possibly a danger to Lola. But she wasn't either of those things. Her spoiled rich girl exterior had gotten under his skin, but she was much more than that.

"And we're consenting adults." He started, realizing that he'd been staring at her, devouring her with his eyes like a fucking creep. "At least I'm consenting."

"Consenting to what?" She couldn't possibly see inside his mind. He wanted her to take his cock in her mouth far enough that tears ran down her face. He wanted to fuck her so many times that she'd remember him inside her every time she moved for a month. He wanted to make her mouth swollen with kisses and leave fingerprint bruises on her inner thighs from holding her legs open so he could eat her up until she lost herself in pleasure, again and again.

He was sick with how much he wanted her and how swiftly she woke up desires he'd thought long dead. Sure, he always liked rough sex. But, even with his other partners, he'd never let himself off the leash the way that he wanted to with Carla. None of them aroused lust that gnawed at his gut and made his skin itch. She was like heroin, not that he would know. But that's how the addicts he'd photographed for a story last year had described it.

How would he put into words what he needed to do to her, and how dangerous it could be for both of them?

"I don't want to hurt you." That was the essence of the issue.

"You think I'm going to catch feelings for you?" She shook her head, her drying hair drifting over her shoulders and arousing a new fantasy of using her ponytail as a steering wheel while he took her from behind. "I'm not. I just want sex. Or rolling around naked. Sucking you off. Or if that doesn't make you comfortable, I'd settle for mutual masturbation."

Her talking about putting her hand on his dick had him feeling the ghost of a touch. Even a hand job from Carla could send him over the edge.

"Why are you pressing the issue?"

It seemed that, despite their proximity, she didn't like him all that much. It was a mystery to him why she was so insistent that they get down and dirty together.

"You're hot."

Women liked him sure, but he was tall and didn't look like someone had taken a shovel to his face. He wasn't vain enough to call himself "hot." "Do you fuck every hot guy you meet? Not that it would matter." Really, not that it *should* matter, but he still wanted to throttle any guy who'd fucked her before. He ought to be ashamed of that, but his carnal need made him feral and territorial.

"No, but I just got dumped. And, even though we don't like each other and don't have anything in common, I want to have sex with you. I want to touch you."

"So, I'd be your rebound." He should be fully onboard with her using him sexually since it aligned with what he could offer her, but something stopped him from grabbing her from the table and taking her to bed immediately. "Why did you two break up?"

She looked down, breaking eye contact with him for the first time. "He said I wasn't exciting enough."

That left him dumbfounded. Since they'd met yesterday, he'd experienced more up and down spikes than were possibly healthy for him and his late-thirties' blood pressure. When she was serving him food or spread out for him to taste, she was so sweet she could give him diabetes. That afternoon, when he'd been worried she'd get caught up in the storm while trying to help people, she'd had his heart rate up so high that he'd felt the blood pounding in his neck. And when she called him out or told him what to do, it made him so hard he could barely stand upright.

"He's an idiot." He knew he was going to regret his words, but he said, "You're right. We need to have sex tonight."

* * * *

This was the weirdest seduction she'd ever performed. She'd had to hector him for fifteen minutes, describe what they would do sans condoms, and finally had to guilt him into fucking her. She ought to be ashamed—especially given how not excited he seemed about having sex with her—but she wasn't.

He had a bite on his way to his mouth when she asked, "Was that a pity orgasm earlier?"

He looked horrified by her question, sort of like he was about to choke. His "What?" was more of a cough than a question.

"Did you go down on me because you felt bad that I had a panic attack?"

"No." He dropped his fork. "If anything, I only did that much because I was worried you only wanted to hook up because you felt bad that I saw you like that. You seem like someone who cares a lot about what other people think of you."

He was right—about most people. Although she wanted Jonah to like her, particularly with his penis, she didn't really care what he thought of her in a deeper sense. Whether or not he'd thought her motives for coming down to the island were pure didn't really matter, did they? They would never see each other again when they both left this house. He'd go off to some disaster porn hot spot and she'd go back to her little life in Miami.

She'd get her head together and arrange teas with her mother. She'd stand up in her sister's wedding. Maybe someday, she'd find another guy like Geoff, except maybe even less attractive and more staid. Someone who would never think of leaving her and who would think the Junior League was the height of excitement. Someone who would appreciate what she had to offer.

Even thinking it out in her head made her want to cry. How would she go back to that? She didn't know, and she didn't have to think about it right now. The concept of what her life would always be made it even more imperative that she grab the man in front of her with both hands and ring him the fuck out before the storm passed.

"What are you thinking about?"

"You're right. I care way too much about what other people think."

He grabbed her hand, and the heat of his touch traveled through her whole body, torching her old life to pieces. As long as she could remember that this was temporary, everything would be fine. She might have to grit her teeth and endure for the rest of her life, but she had it a lot better than most. Because of her family, she should never have to worry about money. She had a very nice roof over her head, a closet full of designer clothes, and people who tolerated her—nay, loved her—despite her shallowness and shortcomings. That should be enough. That would have to be enough.

"I don't want to care what you think of me, but it bothers me that you don't approve of me. I don't know why. No one in my family thinks I have much to offer, but I want you to see me." Saying it out loud was terrifying, but it felt vitally important. Somehow, in falling apart in front of him and cajoling him into having sex with her, she'd stumbled into something intense and emotional. If only if it weren't so damned fleeting.

The look in his olive-green eyes melted her reticence about opening up to him. She wished they had more time. The way he looked at her right now was everything. The little huffs of breath between them, seated around one corner of the massive table, the only audible sounds inside the house. The wind might scream outside, debris hitting buildings and trees, and the rain pelting the stone masonry of the house hushed the noise inside her head and focused everything on him.

"I approve of you." His words were a low whisper, and she drank them in like they were sacred wine. "I was wrong about you when you showed up. I still think a romper is a dumb outfit to travel in. I mean how do you use the bathroom on the plane?"

"I flew a private charter. The bathrooms are very nice." She bit her bottom lip, wondering if he would give her shit about her privilege. She would have flown commercial, but she wasn't going to turn down a private plane from her dad. She wasn't dumb.

The corners of his eyes crinkled, and she felt lit up inside. When he smiled every molecule in her body shed the heavy weight of fear. She wanted to bask in his smile forever, taking breaks only the revel and whirl in his desire for her.

"What are you thinking about?" She had to know if he was regretting being stuck here with her. She needed to know if he thought she was silly.

"Only you could make the argument for the practicality of a private plane."

"The bathrooms are bigger, too." She ran her fingers up his arm, over his shoulder. "You probably have a problem fitting inside a plane bathroom."

"Let's just say I'm not a member of the mile-high club." If she could ever get with him on a private plane, she would most definitely remedy that immediately. It wouldn't happen, but it was a useful fantasy to have in her arsenal for the trip home.

"You don't think I'm spoiled?"

"I do." That almost broke the spell; it felt like a betrayal after his kind look and previous words. Before she could respond angrily, he said, "But I don't think you're spoiled in a bad way. I think you're loved, and that's a good thing. Not everyone gets it."

All of the sudden, she realized she knew next to nothing about him and his past. "Did you not have it?"

He looked away from her, down at his plate, and she drew her hand away when his body went stiff and cold. Maybe he didn't have a place to call home, and that's why he traveled so much. Maybe no one loved him enough to worry about him, so it didn't matter to him whether he was in harm's way all the time. She absolutely hated the thought of him getting himself blown up, contracting some terrible disease or something because he didn't have anyone. It broke her heart, like actually pierced her chest cavity and made her ache.

"My mom loved me."

"She's not here anymore?"

He shook his head.

How long?"

"A long time." He looked at her again, his emotional depths closed to her. He'd replaced them with lust. "But talking about my dead mom isn't going to get you rebound sex, is it?"

Chapter 10

Jonah did not want to talk about his mother or about how he'd disappointed her so badly that she'd dropped dead.

Now that he was clear on the fact that she wanted to fuck him because she was interested in his body—not fill up some emotional hole—he wanted that. Talking about his past would only make that difficult.

Her face was crumpled with concern, and he knew his sharp left turn into DTFville had thrown her for a loop. He opened his mouth, ready to take back his words, and say something mature when she said, "You don't have to tell me if it hurts. You can, but you don't have to. Just try to be kind."

"I can do that." Both their plates were empty, so he stood and took them to the sink. It would be good to rinse them while they still had running water. "I didn't mean to turn into a douchebag, but I don't like talking about my family."

"I feel like my family are the only thing I ever talk about."

"Are they assholes?" It seemed to him like any family that would peg someone as dynamic as Carla as the family screw-up had vision problems or something.

"They're not assholes, but my brother and sister are really smart. They both went to big schools, and they're good with things like numbers and spreadsheets." She sighed and leaned her hip on the counter next to him. "I don't have any skills that help the family business, so I help where I can."

"That doesn't mean you need to stay the same for the rest of your life." He kind of hated her family for pushing her into marriage with a guy who couldn't see her. But then he flashed back to the first time he'd seen her. He was good at his job because he routinely looked past the surface of government propaganda and public relations bullshit to get to the gritty underbelly. He hadn't done that with her right away, and maybe her family hadn't done that ever. "Do you ever travel?"

"I'm traveling right now." She snorted out a laugh, another thing he found endearing about her. "It's not going so well."

"Sorry you're stuck here with me." He knew he was a surly asshole, and he'd closed up on her pretty tight when she'd asked about his family.

"That's not what I mean." She laid her hand on his arm again. When she'd done it at the table, he'd thought of a name for that move: "the soothe the savage beast." The instant her skin touched his, his heartbeat evened out. It was still fast because her touch shifted the ground under him, but each beat had a purpose when they made contact. That purpose was entirely prurient, each movement of his arteries and veins wanting him to get inside her, to clutch at her, taste her until they were both wrung out.

"I'm not 'stuck here' with you. That's not what I meant." She moved behind him and pressed her body up against his. He sighed and hung his head, his hands still in soapy water. He loved having her touch him, moving first. Then, he could be sure that she wanted him, that she craved contact with him as much as he wanted it with her. "You worry a lot about offending people for a journalist. Aren't you supposed to be pushy and dogged in the pursuit of the truth?"

"I am, but I don't want to push you around. I'm big, and I just want to make sure you're never doing something because you're afraid of me."

"Why would I be afraid of you?" She laid her lips on his midback, and his skin felt the burn from beneath his shirt. "Is it because you're six and a half feet tall, jacked to Jesus, and you rarely smile?"

"That's enough to make most people afraid." And after what had happened in college, anyone with Google was leery of him. That's why he liked being out of country. People didn't know about his past. As long as he was careful and spoke softly enough, they tended to open up to him. That's why he got the shots he was able to get and why he'd been a finalist for a Pulitzer last year for the photo he took of a group of orphans in Aleppo. He didn't want the awards for the publicity, but they were useful in getting him the kind of jobs that made the world *look* at what was going on, the kind of photos you couldn't look away from.

"After you carried me almost a mile through the streets of Havana and made me come so hard I almost cried, I'm not afraid of you." She moved her hands from his biceps, under his arms, and caressed his stomach. "The way you interrogated my wanting to be with you more than any man ever had."

"I didn't interrogate you."

"You could write a fucking manual on enthusiastic consent."

"What's that?"

"It's not just saying yes to sex to make someone else happy. It's doing it because you want it. Like, I think you want me to touch you because your skin raises goose bumps when I do. But I don't know if you're scared of me."

"I'm not scared of you."

"Good." She dipped her hands and tickled him beneath his T-shirt. He wasn't ticklish, but it made it impossible to remember whether he'd rinsed the dishes. She unbuttoned his jeans and asked, "Do I have your 'enthusiastic consent' to give you hand job?"

Fuck. Fuck, yes. "Please."

She pushed his pants and boxer briefs down around his thighs, and he flattened his palms on the counter on either side of the sink when she encircled him as much as she could with her one hand. When she wet the other in the suds still circling the sink, his balls went heavy.

She grabbed him with both hands, stroking him off in rhythm. Where he was afraid to handle her too roughly, Carla handled him with more force than he would have thought her capable. The pressure and tempo were just right. He could feel her breathe hard from the effort of stretching her arms around his torso and moving in a way that pleased him. He should turn around and give her more space, but this felt too good for him to move.

His usual stance on hand jobs was that they were overrated. But he'd never been touched like this before. Usually, there were a lot of other areas to explore. But tonight, without the requisite supplies, touching and stroking was all there was.

He fucked her hand, growing close to out of control. "I can feel your gorgeous little tits against my back. I want to fuck them." At that moment he didn't care how porny that was.

"What else?" No recriminations, no ick factor. She was down for whatever, and it only made her hotter.

"If I can't get inside you, I want you to swallow me, take me in."

"You think I can swallow this whole thing?"

"*Yes.*" And she gripped him even tighter, and sped up.

"I think so, too. I can't wait to get my mouth on you. I'm tempted to do it right now." Even though he wasn't touching her, her voice was needy and desperate, as if she was getting fucked.

"Don't fucking move." If she stopped touching him now, he'd have a heart attack. She could certainly give a guy a stroke from stopping *this stroke*. Fucking genius she was.

While he spun fantasies—made plans—about what he'd do to her tonight, his orgasm snuck up on him. Everything narrowed down to her hands and his cock, her smooth motions driving him crazier by the minute.

"Fuck, Carla. That's so fucking good. You're so fucking good." When he came, he bent at the waist, and her hands popped off his cock. He was so sensitive, but he wanted her touch back. When he turned to find her fully clothed, he suddenly felt vulnerable.

He let his jeans fall—he wouldn't be wearing pants for the rest of the night and maybe not the next day if they didn't have to see to storm damage, but he rucked his boxer briefs up. She was still fully clothed after all.

He was about to tell her to take off her clothes so he could taste all of her skin until she recovered when she looked down at her hands, covered in him.

"You wanted me to taste you." She stuck her index finger in her mouth, licking it clean. He was half-hard again. "Think I'll get a preview."

He closed the small space between them and tugged her shirt up until she had to drop her arms. "You're wearing too many clothes, princess." She grunted when her head popped free of her T-shirt. "There they are."

The teasing, bouncing pair that tortured his mind and dominated his thoughts were hard-tipped and pointed at him. He took a nipple between two fingers and squeezed. Carla's mouth popped open, and "More" came out with a pant.

He squeezed harder, used his other hand to give her other nipple the same treatment, and her head fell back.

"Unzip those little cock-tease shorts if you want more." She fumbled but unzipped and pushed the shorts and her panties down. She'd broken down his control, and he wanted to do the same for her. He wanted her to be as dependent on his touch as he was on hers. Seeing her rush to obey him gratified him because it meant he was giving her the gift she'd given him. "I didn't say to take off your panties."

"But—" Her words broke off into a moan when he pinched harder. He released both nipples then closed the space between them. Feeling her skin all up against his for the first time made him want to growl. She hissed in pleasure and scored his ribs with her fingernails.

He bent until his mouth was next to her ear. "Be careful, princess. You're turning me into a wild man."

He wrapped his arms around her, grabbing both ass cheeks. "I want that."

"What do you want? You want to turn me into a wild man?" He slapped one cheek, and she yelped. "You want me to eat you all up?" He slapped the other cheek, and she sighed and fell against him, but she didn't answer his questions. "You're going to need to answer me. I need that *enthusiastic* consent."

"If I were any more enthusiastic, I'd be dead."

"Sarcastic." She nodded sleepily and burrowed closer to him; her fingers played in his chest hair. "You seemed to like it when I talked about spanking you. Are you aiming to get spanked by being sarcastic?"

"Maybe."

He grabbed her hips and moved her away from him. She was a tiny Venus, curvy and delicious. The freckles were everywhere, but they were more prominent on her shoulders and upper back. He pushed his fingers into her skin. "Do you like playing rough, princess?"

Her green eyes went liquid and unfocused as he increased his pressure, telling him she did. But he wanted to hear the words.

"Yes. I mean, I think so. I like whatever you're doing to me."

"You want me to spank you." He stroked one hand up the side of her body, tracing her form, committing it to memory. "You have to tell me what you want so that I don't hurt you." He squeezed her whole breast. It fit in his hand. She stood on her tiptoes and leaned in.

"I want it to hurt. I know you won't injure me. I want to feel more with you."

That's all he needed to hear. He turned her around and bent her body against the counter.

"You ready?"

* * * *

The tile was cold against Carla's breasts, but everything else was hot. The heavy palm of one hand against the back of her neck, tangled up in her hair. The places where his fingers had dug into her skin tingled as if he still touched her. Even the skin on her ass cheeks burned with anticipation, as though they were warmed up and waiting for a thundering smack from his hand.

She didn't know why she wanted this from him, but she needed it. Although she loved the way he'd let her have her way with him—touching him at will had filled her with pleasure—this waiting for him, giving over to him, was everything.

He had her under his control, and she didn't have to worry about anything except for his next touch. And she didn't have to worry about that because she would feel something, and he was always giving her more.

Where he'd been skillful and aggressive during the afternoon, this was special. Their desire had twisted somehow, morphed into something more. He didn't leave her hanging for too long, just waited enough for her to sweat, to feel the air against her center, and get even more turned on by the waiting energy.

His first slap was light, but it made her sway and slide over the counter;

his anchoring hand and her locking her knees were the only things that kept her in place. Her flesh burned even brighter and she clenched around the air. She turned her head in his light grasp and moaned into the counter.

After earlier today and right now, it was a good thing the tiling was going to be replaced. She'd never be able to look at this kitchen without blushing. Worse yet, she would never be able to look at this kitchen without longing for the freedom she felt right now with this man.

He spanked her again. "All right?" The force of his palm against her coupled with checking in made her feel so safe, so cared for.

She wanted to scream, "You're not going to hurt me!" Instead, she nodded and purred out something that she hoped sounded like "Yes. Yes. Yes."

Even though she knew it couldn't happen, she wanted his cock inside her so much. After holding his girth in her hands, she would never be able to get the idea of fucking him to leave her brain.

He stopped spanking her, and she pushed her butt into the air. It was too soon. She needed more, and he couldn't just stop like this. His hand on her neck didn't move, but he ran two fingers over her clit. She arched her back, wanting more.

"What do you need? You want my fingers inside or outside?"

"Both."

"Greedy girl." She heard the amusement in his voice, so she knew he didn't mean it literally. But she was greedy for him. He was in short supply, and she demanded as much of him as she could afford. He penetrated her with one finger, and they both cursed at the pleasure of it. "Such a sweet, tight grip, princess."

"Yes." She arched back in time to the thrust of his hand. He had one fingertip on her clit that set her on fire with every stroke. He added another finger, and sweat started rolling down her face onto the counter. The contact point between her neck and his hand started sliding around, adding more delicious friction until he moved his palm down her spine, holding onto her lower back so he could get more leverage.

It might only be his fingers, but there was no mistaking the fact that she was being *fucked*.

She wanted him to never stop, and he didn't, even when an orgasm broke her apart. His fingers didn't have a refractory period, and when it came to him, she didn't either. He kept on, until his arms must have tired, but she came again. When she did, when fire rocked through her entire body, and she'd surely turned into a puddle of thoroughly fucked woman, he withdrew.

They both slid to the floor, skin sticking to each other and the cabinets.

She kissed his pectoral, and he sighed with contentment.

His hand moved up and down her back, and she would have fallen asleep there.

"We should get up."

"I don't want to." She wanted to stay right where she was, separating from him was unthinkable.

But the storm didn't care what she wanted. The branches from the palm trees in the courtyard thwacked against the outer walls of the house, beating at the weathered stucco. The heavy rain echoed against metal gutters outside.

"If the lights go out, I don't want us fumbling around down here in the dark."

He had a point, but she still wasn't convinced. So, she didn't move. She breathed the smell of their mingled sweat in, and she ran her mouth back and forth over his nipple with her arms wrapped around him. She smiled—inside and out—with her whole body. When she closed her eyes, her cheeks warmed at how much he made her feel.

"I don't care. I can't let this go right now."

He seemed to understand that because he closed his arms around her and squeezed. Carla was an affectionate person. She'd missed touching someone, having someone to touch, in the past few months. Yesterday, she never would have thought that she would be cuddled up to Jonah, but it felt right today. She was going to embrace it while she could.

A few minutes in to their cuddle-fest, something from outside crashed into one of the boards covering the window over the sink, and the glass shattered. She didn't feel any glass hit her because Jonah had moved so quickly to cover her body.

With him holding her, she didn't panic. Everything inside her went still, and she waited for him.

"Where are your shoes?" She looked around. She'd kicked them off earlier, while they were eating, so they were out of reach.

"Shit."

She looked down at his bare feet. "You don't have any shoes either."

"Yeah, but my tetanus shots are up-to-date."

She supposed they would have to be, given his profession. The reminder that he was always in danger was more of a shock to the system than the broken window had been. She'd never forgotten the storm completely, but she'd been able to put Jonah's job out of her head when his hand had been between her legs.

When she reached to lever herself up on the counter, he grabbed her hands. "The glass blew everywhere."

"Both of us are going to get cut. There's no way of avoiding it."

He grunted, and the floor disappeared beneath her as he lifted her up on his shoulder and stood. She'd been impressed when he'd carried her almost a mile. She was small, but not that small. This here was some superhuman shit. It turned her on, even though it was kind of fucked up that it did. But everything about him was a turn on to her, what was she supposed to do? Deny it?

"You're going to get your feet all cut up."

"Stop wiggling."

He passed through the threshold into the dining room where, from her vantage point, there didn't seem to be any glass on the ground.

"I'll stop wiggling when you put me down."

"There could still be glass."

"There aren't any windows broken in here."

"Why are you arguing with me?"

"You don't have to carry me." She liked him carrying her, but she didn't *need* it. "You can put me down anytime."

"I like carrying you, though." So much blood rushed to her head that she couldn't have heard him right.

"Why?" He got to the stairs, and the ride got bouncier. "At least let me get upright."

"No."

"Why not?"

He slapped her ass, shocking her. "I like the view here."

To be honest, her view didn't entirely suck either. Still, out of retaliation, she slapped his boxer-brief-covered ass back so hard her hand stung.

"Violence is never the answer, princess."

Chapter 11

Jonah didn't want to admit that Carla was right. He did get his feet all cut up. Not badly enough that he needed stitches, but badly enough that she had to go hunting in her great aunt's bathroom for a first aid kit.

He'd brought her to her room, and he'd intended to give her some space to process what had happened downstairs. Hell, he needed space to get his head screwed on right. Even thinking the word *screwed* had his cock filling with blood. Thinking about anything that could even be tangentially related to sex around Carla was hazardous to his cock.

But, given the fact that the tile floor in Carla's room looked like a crime scene, he'd sat on her bed when she'd ordered him to. While she was out of the room, he tried to fast-track his thought process.

Carla had knocked him on his ass. He hadn't expected her, but he was grateful they were stuck here together. Maybe, when she was home and he took a trip stateside, they could see each other again. He'd just have to make that happen because not having her ride him while pinching her sweet nipples until she panted was no longer an option. He needed to have her, and he didn't want to think about never having the opportunity to be inside her.

She had him so filled with adrenaline that he didn't even feel the pain of his injuries. He'd almost forgotten about them when she walked in with a first-aid kit—and a box that looked like a condom box but couldn't possibly a box of condoms.

The saucy smile on her face told him that he might not be hallucinating. He started to stand before he remembered himself.

"Is that what I think it is?"

"You'll sit down and let me fix your feet if you want to find out."

"Yes, ma'am."

He plopped back down on the bed and she knelt in front of him, which did not help him stop thinking about that box of condoms.

She looked up at him, the Devil dancing in her eyes. "Stop thinking about putting that big cock in my mouth." The cock in question wanted to be right there, between her soft lips.

"So that's off the table now that there are condoms?"

"No, but you're bleeding. I'm not going to give you a blow job while you're bleeding all over the floor." She lifted his foot and doused it with antiseptic spray. He winced at the burn, pulling his foot back in. Carla tugged back. "If you can't act like a big boy, fellatio is indeed off the table." That made him stop fighting her touch.

She looked at the soles of his feet and grimaced. "You don't have too many splinters." She picked up a set of tweezers. He wondered if they could still use those condoms if she saw him cry like a toddler. "Good thing you have tough soles."

She'd thrown on a T-shirt that barely covered her ass before she'd gone for the medical supplies. "It would help if you took your top off while performing surgery. I need a distraction."

"Remember what I said about being a big boy?" She leveled a brief glare at him that would make his third grade teacher proud before returning to her task. She was gentle and deft in her movements. Each splinter she pulled out only stung a bit.

"How did you get so good at first aid?"

"I thought I wanted to be a nurse for a hot minute."

"You did—ouch—really?"

"Yeah, but like I said, I'm not very good at math. I couldn't keep up in the first-level classes."

"So you became an interior designer?"

She nodded, pursing her lips before pulling out another shard. "There's really not enough light in here to do this. I hope I can get it all."

"You like your job."

"I do." She spread her hand over her stomach in a gesture of self-defense. "I'm sure you think it's dumb and unnecessary. Why make places beautiful when there's real suffering in the world?"

Before spending time with Carla, he would have dismissed her career as something people with nothing important to do did—like wedding photographers. But he was really curious. Why would someone like Carla—someone with brains and organizational talent—want to haul a trunk full of fabric swatches around instead of helping people?

"I don't think you do it for a frivolous reason."

"You don't?" She stopped, tweezers poised. "I think people deserve to live in beautiful places. I think it helps people get through the real difficulties of life to have an orderly, aesthetically pleasing place to come home to after being out in the world."

That made him think about his apartment in New York. It was tiny, dingy, and he was barely ever there. When he was home—if he could indeed call it that—he was itching to leave almost as soon as he sat on his tattered couch. He had nothing there. No one to share it with. "I can see what you mean."

"All done with that one." She switched feet and came at him with the Satan-spawned antiseptic again. This time, he closed his eyes and imagined sucking on her nipples while she rode him. "You're being a very good patient. You are so going to get a treat for this."

"Am I?" He bit his bottom lip as she tugged a shard of glass out of the ball of his foot. It stung like a bitch. "You know you'd be a lot more convincing if you were wearing a candy-striper uniform."

"Oh, you have a thing for caregivers, do you?" He opened his eyes in time to see her smile at him, raising one eyebrow. "You want a sponge bath after we're done here?"

He shook his head, needing her to be done as soon as possible. "No, I have plans for that box." He tipped his chin at the nightstand, grinning back at her.

"Well, for now, lie back and think of England."

* * * *

When she got the last of the glass out of Jonah's foot, she thought about trying to find a mop to clean up the blood all over the floor for about a few seconds. Just until he pulled her up onto the bed with him. In the process, her T-shirt hiked up, and his hands moved under it, caressing her lower back.

He could turn her on without even making it look like trying. The barest of touches and she softened and opened for him. The idea that she would get to feel him inside her soon had her squirming against him.

Thank goodness for her great aunt's hopping sex life. She'd done a gleeful little dance, cutting it short only to dig bloody glass out of Jonah's foot. It would be hard for him to fuck her all night if any of his wounds got infected. Gangrene wasn't sexy at all.

"You want to get up and get those condoms so I can have my treat?" The smile in his voice was infectious. She winked at him.

"I was thinking more along the lines of a lollipop." He flipped her over on her back and tugged her top the rest of the way off. She palmed his cock through his boxers, feeling a damp spot on the fabric. He grunted. "Did getting glass pulled out of your foot turn you on? You're a dirtier boy than I thought."

"I did what you told me to do. I might have been lying down, but I was most certainly not thinking of England."

She spread her legs, making room for his hips. He pumped against her, his frame moving smoothly, seemingly without effort. He might be a big guy, but he wasn't a lunk by any means. He reminded her of a tiger. Sleek and large. Even though he'd done everything he could to make her comfortable, there was nothing domesticated about him.

"What were you thinking about?" She'd barely got the question out before he brushed his still-clothed cock against her bare clit. She gasped, still sensitive. But she wanted more. She felt like she'd been asleep below the belt for years. Now that she was awake, she wanted to gorge on this man. She might be greedy, and she might have eyes bigger than her vagina, but she didn't care.

"I wasn't thinking about dry humping you."

"Then why are we wasting time on this?" He ground into her, and she made an *eep* sound.

"You call this a waste of time? I wish I had all the time in the world to show how I'd like to waste your time."

She didn't even resent the reminder that they were only a temporary thing because it got her to push at his shoulders. "I think we need those condoms now."

Almost reluctantly, he rolled to his side. When she got off the bed, she could feel him scrutinizing her ass. He was so an ass man. She put an extra bit of sway in her step on the way to the nightstand, moving slowly. But she took a running jump to get back to him.

He caught her and set her on the bed beside him.

She tore the plastic off the box like she'd torn the paper off her Teletubbies dolls at age four. She might not have been this excited since then. Not when she'd made her debut, not when she'd graduated from college, not even when she'd gotten engaged.

The idea that she was going to get to have sex with Jonah Kane after laboring under the belief that fingering was as good as it got was quite possibly the best thing to ever happen to her. He might not share it as a pinnacle experience. Hell, he'd probably peaked Everest and Kilimanjaro. His life was all excitement, all the time. But, when he nearly shredded his boxer briefs while removing them, she reminded herself that she was probably a peak experience for his dick. And that would just have to be enough.

She sat facing him while applying the condom, carefully. They should probably use the large size, but it covered most of it. And that would have to do.

He grunted in frustration at her taking her time. He looked at the strip of uncovered flesh and said, "I don't have anything. I get checked a lot because of all the travel. My last test is recent."

"Neither do I, but I'm not on birth control." They'd talked about everything else sexual, so this conversation was easy-peasy. "It's not the right time, but we should still use these."

"Of course. I've never fucked anyone without a condom." Of course he hadn't. That just wasn't how Jonah rolled. He demanded enthusiastic consent before engaging in all variety of filthy and depraved acts on kitchen counters and floors. He was a pervert with a heart of gold. A pussy pirate with a code. She laughed. "Are you laughing at safe sex?"

"No, I was thinking about fucking you if you had an eye patch and a peg leg."

"Well, you saved me from gangrene, so the peg leg isn't likely." She ran her finger over the scar running through his brow. "The eye patch could probably be arranged."

The "if we had more time" was implied.

"I don't think we need the eye patch."

"Argh, matey." He smiled and she cackled.

"Stop that. She's going to dry up if you call her matey."

"Who's going to dry up?" He pushed her back on the bed and scooted down her body. "Your pussy likes me too much to dry up from a bad joke. And she is my little matey." He was right. Nothing he said was turning her off.

"I think I liked it better when you were calling me princess."

She looked down her body to where he was poised between her legs. He moved them wider, wide enough for his hips, before swooping down for another kiss.

They definitely hadn't kissed enough because she could never get enough of kissing him. His mouth could do pornographic things to her mouth just as deftly as it had made his "little matey" into his love slave.

The lights flickered and went out, but he didn't stop. It was full dark, and with nothing left to do but feel him moving against her, they toggled from joking to deadly serious desire in a matter of seconds.

He hovered at her entrance, waiting for her to welcome him inside. From holding it in her hand and sneaking stares at his hard-on all night, she knew it was big. But neither of those things prepared her for how full he would make her feel when he was all the way inside her.

He wasn't just having sex with her there; he was inside her everywhere. It was so overwhelming she was thankful that he stayed still for a few moments, until she arched her back and pumped her hips using the leverage of her heels on the bed.

"See, your pussy likes me, princess." He pulled out, and her muscles went lax. "That's it." He pushed back inside her and stayed again. "She's been wanting this since I opened that door."

"So cocky, Jonah." She couldn't deny it now that his cock moved inside her so perfectly. "You are definitely a pirate."

He grabbed her backside. "I'm definitely all about this booty."

Her laugh was caught short when he pumped inside her from a new angle. "Stop joking and do that again."

"Princess, I can do both at the same time. I'm a multitasker." On the next stroke, his pelvic bone hit her clit and she choked on her snarky come back. "How about you multitask and rub your clit for me."

"Ay, Ay, Captain."

She did as she was told, and she clenched around him. She felt like her cells were rearranging themselves around him with every stroke. It wasn't an out-of-body experience. She was right there, and she felt everything. But sex with Jonah was otherworldly.

Something inside him shifted because his strokes became less calculated and more instinctive. They might be in the missionary position, but there was nothing boring about what they were doing right now.

She wrapped each leg around one of his, needing to keep him closer to her. Between their bodies, she rubbed herself harder and faster, needing this orgasm more than she'd needed the previous ones. He followed her lead and stroked harder and faster until they were both panting.

He muttered words like *perfect, beautiful, princess, yes*. And when she came, the cells that he'd moved around didn't fall back together like they had been before. Watching him come and tell her she was amazing changed their configuration forever.

Chapter 12

Jonah had never been much of a joker during sex. The last straw with Shannon had been his supposed lack of a sense of humor. So, laughing and fucking at the same time had never happened to him before.

The jokes, laughing while he was close to coming were a revelation. He wrapped his fingers around the condom as he pulled out and disposed of it quickly in the bathroom closest to Carla's bedroom. The soles of his feet stung, but the rest of his body felt too good for him to really care.

He hoped she would be okay with him bunking with her. He could stretch the truth and say he didn't want to be in another room in case one of the windows facing the courtyard broke, but he didn't want to be a room away when he needed her body again. And he would need her again before the night was out.

And after tonight, before they both left the island, he was going to find a way to convince her to see him again. Him in New York and her in Miami wasn't ideal; his travel made the whole long-distance thing pretty impossible. But they could work something out. She'd just gotten out of a long-term relationship; surely she'd want to keep things casual for a while at least.

All of his relationships had been based on common experience and proximity. Carla lived a life that he wasn't sure he could fit himself into, and she certainly wouldn't want to pack her bags and go on the road with him. He shuddered when he thought about her in a conflict zone; he would never allow it.

But he was willing to face some inconvenience so she wouldn't walk out of his life forever. He'd hold onto her for as long as he could before she inevitably cut him loose.

When he walked back into the room, Carla's hair was splayed out across her pillow. She was on her side, facing him, and she didn't hide her appreciation for his body one bit as he walked toward her. He'd always thought his size made him a freak show that women sometimes had a fetish for. It was clear that Carla had a fetish, but it wasn't for his size. She maybe had a burgeoning fetish for him.

"Seen enough?"

"Never." She buried her face in the pillow and sighed before nodding at the box of condoms. "There's eleven more. Do you think we can use them all before the storm passes?"

He pretended to consider her challenge, but he'd already been thinking the same thing. "Would I have to give up my blow job?"

She mocked seriousness. "That's between you and your dick. It's none of my business."

He crawled onto the bed, so he was crouched over her, no longer worried that his size intimidated her. "My dick is very much your business." He laid kisses on her cheeks and nose, softly. He wanted to eat her peals of laughter as a midnight snack. He wanted to bottle up the sound and take it with him.

He would only bring it out when he was alone in dark places. When he needed her light the most.

* * * *

Five down. Seven to go. Carla felt every single one of those five times Jonah had been inside her the night before. After the first time that had shifted her reality, they'd had slow, soft sex.

Then they'd fought about music. He had given her a world of shit for liking One Direction and had called Harry Styles a pansy. She'd told him that she'd gone to Coachella and Austin City Limits, and he'd correctly pointed out that she'd used it like a fashion show. He'd listed off a bunch of artists he loved and she'd never heard of. When she'd rolled her eyes at him, he'd taken her from behind.

That time had led to her sucking him off until he'd cursed and pulled her hair. She'd loved making him feel that out of control, so she rode him while he steered her hips. That had been a fight for control; she'd loved every minute.

The fifth time, he'd woken her up kissing the back of her neck. He'd pulled her hair—who knew she'd like that so much—until she begged him to fuck her. He'd hiked up her leg and pulled it over his body, which allowed him to rub her center and left her helpless to do anything but moan and praise him.

So, they'd made a good run of using the entire box of condoms before they'd gone to sleep. But, judging from the beams of sunlight peeking around the plywood covering the windows, they hadn't beaten the storm. They needed to be outside, helping with cleanup.

Jonah was curled behind her snoring, something she would have abhorred in a long-term partner but found charming in her temporary paramour. She lifted one hand to her neck, feeling where he'd made marks on her body. The last time he'd come, he bit into the tendon at the side. He probably hadn't realized that he would leave a mark, but she'd swatted him on the ass as soon as he'd turned over to get her water.

Judging from the number of empty bottles, Lola was going to have to stock up again as soon as she got back.

Thinking about Lola made Carla sit up straight in the bed. Jonah stirred, but he rolled to his back. She poked him in the side.

"Lola."

He stirred again and rubbed one massive hand over his eyes. "What? Is she here?"

"No. We have to find her."

"She's a smart lady; you know she found shelter."

"No, I don't know that. For someone who professes to care about my great aunt, you sure are lackadaisical about her safety."

"Hey." He was fully awake now—and pissed. "That's not fair. She's not a delicate flower." The "like you" he left unsaid. "She's a tough bird, and she's fine. I know it."

"You sound really sure." Carla gathered up the sheet. She didn't want to be naked in front of Jonah when they were arguing. Then, he might realize that arguing with him made her nipples hard. "You think you're invincible and people like you are invincible."

"I've seen my friends blown up."

"So, why are you so sure that Lola is 'just fine'?"

"Because she has to be, all right?" He rubbed his eyes again with the heels of his hands. "I couldn't take it if I was selfish—here with you—if she was out there suffering. She has to be all right for what happened last night to be okay."

"What are you talking about?" He was so maudlin that she wanted to ask him if he was on his period. But she didn't because she hated giving men a reason to think that women were somehow less than because of their female bodies. But, seeing him now, 90 percent of the female population would agree that "manstruation" was a thing.

He got up and stomped out of the room, naked. The worst part was that his butt still looked so good she wanted to bite it. She used the facilities, delighted that the toilet still flushed, and got dressed. Although she put on full-length jeans and a T-shirt in an effort to be sensible, she refused to admit that she did so hoping that Jonah wouldn't make fun of her clothes again. If he was moody and hormonal, that was his problem.

She was kind of glad that Jonah had decided to be an asshole about last night. That way, she could remember the sex fondly and then stamp out any emotions she felt toward him once she put her battery-operated boyfriend away. Jonah would be like a fantasy dick in a glass case. She'd try not to think about him unless things were really desperate.

She made her way to the top of the stairs, and was about to go down, when Jonah snagged her by the waist. "Go put on a pair of boots."

"I don't have boots."

"Sneakers then."

He was right. She shouldn't be wearing sandals. At this point, she did not want him touching her long enough to pull glass out of her feet. So sandals were out.

Jonah was downstairs by the time she had her sneakers on. He had opened the front door, which they hadn't put plywood over—it was crazy heavy—and he was on a satellite phone looking out into the street.

She wanted to see the damage for herself—the storm had certainly sounded horrendous from what she'd caught when Jonah wasn't balls deep—but she didn't want to touch him right now.

He was speaking in rapid Spanish to someone, looking for Lola from the sound of the conversation. That made her feel a bit better. He had taken her concerns seriously, and he was dealing with them sensibly.

She didn't know what to do, so she found a broom and dustpan and swept up the glass in the kitchen. After that, she'd bring the mop upstairs and make sure all the blood was wiped up. Hopefully, Lola would be home soon, and she wasn't sure how she'd explain bloodstains, unless she actually killed Jonah and made even more. Lola might not forgive her for that.

He came into the kitchen and grabbed the broom out of her hands. "What are you doing?"

"I don't want you to get cut."

"I can take care of myself." She looked down at his boot-clad feet. "I know first aid."

Trying to say the conversation was closed with a stubborn tip of her chin didn't work. "I know you can take care of yourself. Thank you for taking care of me last night." He set the broom and dustpan aside and grabbed her shoulders. She tried to shrug him off. For the first time since she'd known him, he touched her without her permission. "You have to know I'm sorry. I'm a grumpy asshole, and I'm sorry."

He immediately released her, and she missed his hands, wanted them back.

"Okay." He looked at her expectantly, like she had something to apologize for. "What do you want?"

"I just thought you'd want to talk about what happened last night." Cocky Jonah was back as he gathered up his hair and tied it in a knot. *Fucking cocky Jonah.* She wanted to choke cocky Jonah out while riding him. "You're thinking about when I touched you in your no-no place right now, aren't you?" She tried to keep a scowl on her face.

"Fuck you." She crossed her arms over her chest, afraid her nipples would bust the fabric on her bra just to get to him. "You were on the phone, looking for Lola. Where is she?"

He leaned one hip onto the countertop, the one she was going to have to remove with the sledgehammer before Lola got home, and she assumed that her great aunt was coming home because Jonah was cocky Jonah with the sex jokes right now.

"All it took was one phone call. She's fine. She and her boy toy holed up at a friend's place on high ground. Apparently they played jazz, danced, and drank rum all night. She'll be home in a few days."

"Thank you."

"For what? One phone call. You know I was just as worried about her as you were?"

"You were?" She scrunched up her face and peered up at him. "From where I was sitting, you were in denial, getting all fucking emo when I was actually worried sick."

"You can't wake me up with disaster scenarios and expect me to take that shit well." She was chastened because she was probably being unfair. "That's just not how I operate. If we're going to—"

Though he cut himself off, the start of that sentence gave her a kind of hope she wasn't even sure she wanted to feel. Did he want to see her after he left the island? Was he going to try to make them a thing?

Despite the fact that she was trying to talk herself out of having feelings for him, part of her really wanted him to try to make them a thing.

"What were you going to say?" Hope did a dance in her chest.

He examined her face, leaning down as though he was going to kiss her. "Never mind."

And then he walked out of the room.

Chapter 13

Jonah needed to get the fuck out of here. Like the first flight. He couldn't—wouldn't—spend any more time with Carla conjuring up her little witch spells. He went up to his room and used the satellite phone to call all his friends on the island to see if he couldn't get a flight out on a supply plane.

He realized how pathetic it was that he was looking for a military-style extraction from a girl. But she'd pissed him off so much that he really didn't care. It was like she could see inside him. He *had* gotten emo about Lola, but not for the reasons she thought. The only other time that he'd let a girl get in the way of his caring for family, that family member had died.

When Carla had woken up in a panic about Lola, he'd flashed back to college—to his mother. And, even though it probably made him naïve, Lola felt more like a mother figure to him than anyone since.

As soon as he woke up from the sex cocoon that he and Carla had created in the midst of the storm, he'd been nut-punched by regret.

He shouldn't have lost himself in Carla at the possible expense of Lola's safety, even if it was Carla—a woman who'd burrowed inside him so far that it would take some pliers to get her out.

"Charlie?" he spat out as soon as his buddy picked up the phone.

"Yeah man. Are you doing okay?"

Jonah didn't know how to answer that question. He was physically safe, but what had happened with Carla had shifted something on his insides. It sounded stupid, and that's not what his buddy meant anyway. "I'm fine. Looking to get off the island, actually."

"Let me see what I can do. Stay close to the phone, and I'll call you back in a couple of hours with some details. Carla need a ride out?"

Jonah wondered if she'd be safe here. Then, he thought about her rich family; her father would get her out of trouble. She was a daddy's girl after all.

"No, just me."

He hung up the phone and turned around. Carla was standing in the threshold to his room.

"You're leaving?"

He nodded. "As soon as I can." He looked toward the phone. "You need to call your parents?"

She stood up straighter, with an imperious tilt to her chin. "Yeah, they're probably worried sick or dealing with the same storm we had to deal with last night."

"It's worth a shot trying to get in touch anyway."

She nodded and approached him, careful not to touch him while reaching for the phone. She gave him a wan smile while she dialed. "It's a wonder I remember any numbers, isn't it?"

Her awkward small talk pissed him off. He'd been inside her a few hours ago, and now she was acting like they were strangers at a cocktail party.

It shouldn't bother him because they were supposed to be one-and-done, but he wanted her again and again. He wished he could go back to a few minutes ago and tell her that he wanted to see her again. But she would probably say no. He wasn't the kind of guy she wanted to be with in the long term. She'd probably go back to Miami and find an accountant just like the one who had dumped her.

"Daddy?"

He hated when grown women called their fathers *daddy*. It was weird and, to him, spoke to some sort of stunted growth. He reminded himself that Carla was a lot younger than him, and she'd been coddled her whole life. Her life hadn't been as hard as his—where he'd been the man of the house from the time he was five.

"I'm fine. Aunt Lola's boarder and I managed just fine." She paused, and he heard a deep voice barking questions at her. His hands fisted, and he wanted to reach through the phone and punch her father for yelling at her that way. "He's fine, Daddy. Good people."

She looked at him then, and he warmed to her despite himself.

"I don't know when planes will be getting out." Another pause, and more barked questions. "I called you before I called the airport. I'm not sure any charters will be flying in for a few days." One more pause, and he heard her father's exasperated sigh through the phone. "I'll call the charter company right now. I know it's going to cost you a lot, but I can't do anything about the original plan now that things are so up in the air after the storm."

She looked down at her lap while her father talked. He could tell she was embarrassed by having him hear this conversation, but he didn't move. As though he could protect her from something, he stood sentry while her father lectured her.

If she were his, if she belonged to him, he would have ripped the phone out of her hands and told her father how she'd helped a bunch of people on the block the day before get ready for the storm, how she'd made sure they had food and driven nails into plywood herself. That man shouldn't be talking to her like a child. And yet, he stood next to her and allowed it because he didn't have a right to step in.

"Everyone's all right? You talked to Alana and Javi?" She twirled the phone cord around her finger, fidgeting. "Can I talk to Mom?"

Her face fell at whatever response came over the line. Jonah itched to grab the phone and tell Carla's dad to get her mother on the phone—like five minutes ago.

"I love you, Daddy." *How? Seriously, how?* "Okay. Bye."

Carla hung up the phone.

"Your dad sounds like a jerk," he said. Not that it was any of his business.

She laughed. "He totally is." She sat cross-legged on his bed, like she belonged there.

He might never see her again, but he needed to make things right between them. "He's going to charter a plane?"

"Yep." She gave him a sheepish smile. "He wasn't mad at me. He was mad at having to spend so much money. He's richer than Croesus, but he will be cheap to the death."

"He still didn't have to be an asshole about it. Not like you summoned the storm on purpose."

Jonah sat on the bed facing her, the phone sitting between them. She moved to get up, but he grabbed one thigh with his hand.

"You probably need to make other calls." She looked down at his half-full duffle bag. "It looks like you're ready to leave."

"Not yet." He let his hand travel up her leg until it was pressed into the crease just near her pussy. Carla's mouth fell open on a needy sigh. "I still have something to do first."

Her eyes had gone glassy, and she wet her lips with her tongue. "We didn't beat the storm." She reached into the pocket opposite his hand and pulled out one of the remaining condoms.

"Doesn't matter, princess." He grabbed it from her and laid it on the nightstand. He moved the phone onto the floor.

She shook her head. "No, it doesn't matter."

He leaned in and kissed her. If they hadn't found the miracle box of condoms, he would have been content kissing and touching her. He was a man of simple needs; he took what the moment gave him and was thankful for that, most of the time. Carla, though? He craved her like a drug. Her mouth against his stirred emotions he'd no longer felt capable of a few days ago.

Before long, he had her laid out, red hair splayed across his duffle bag. He wedged himself between her legs, and she wrapped them around his waist. He was too impatient to get her naked, but he didn't want to stop kissing her. The sense of limited time, that this was the last time washed over him.

He kneeled up. "You're a fucking siren, woman. Take off your shirt." If he didn't get his mouth on her tits immediately, he felt like his chest would break open and his guts would pour out.

"You like it." She sat up enough to take her T-shirt off. At his pleading groan, she said, "You're an addict, in fact." She nodded at him. "Yours, too?"

He pulled the shirt off over the back of his head, pulling his hair to cover his face. When he leaned down, she moved it away, twirling her fingers in the strands like she'd done with the phone cord while she was planning to leave him.

He wanted to be here now, gorged in her beauty and the weird science their chemistry made. But he couldn't get the thought that he would never see her again out of his head. She made him ache, and he didn't know how to make that go away.

Crushing his mouth against hers again, he was gratified by the sigh she breathed into him when their skin made contact. He moved his mouth to her collarbone, memorizing the pattern of her freckles. He tongued his favorites, the ones that led to her fat, pink nipples. When he ran his tongue around one areola, she arched into him, grasping and pulling at his shoulders.

"You taste so good." She still smelled like him, and the scent of their mixed sweat made his need for her so much more urgent. "I want to bottle you up and pour you on pancakes like syrup."

"That's disgusting." She might not like his words, but when she pushed him away, she only did so to unbutton her pants. "Maybe you should shut up while you fuck me."

"We're disgusting together." He flipped the button on his jeans. "It's disgusting how much I want you. And you got turned on cleaning glass out of my feet."

"Only because you were mostly naked." She pushed her jeans and panties down to her ankles. He had his pants and boxers around his ankles, blocked by his shoes. They took each other's shoes off, pulling at laces, and tossing them when they were done.

When they were both naked, she fell on him like she was starving. She kissed his mouth, his chest. And her delicate fingers grasped him everywhere. His stomach bottomed out when she ran them through the hair leading to his cock.

He was so ramped up for her that he wouldn't last long if she gave him the kind of hand job she had last night. She dipped one hand between her legs and used that hand to smooth the way. "Oh. Fuck. Princess."

He didn't even care that she had him by the balls right now.

Above him, she was gorgeous, completely debauched. He'd removed the plywood from his window and opened the shutters. The sun flowing through her hair made her look like a sexy wood nymph. He wanted to close his eyes at the pleasure she gave him with her touch, but he couldn't get enough of her wicked smile or the light against her luminous skin. She was a goddess.

She brought her center up to his cock, and he knew she was ready. He reached for her and pressed a thumb to her clit. She threw her head back and offered her breasts to him so enticingly that he sat up and took what she wanted to give him.

He felt her going wild with his touch, and they strained to come together.

"Condom," he said. He needed to get covered up and inside her as soon as humanly possible.

"Don't move." Her voice was strained as if she was almost there. So, he followed orders and rubbed her clit in time with her movements even though her hand on his cock was about to cut this whole shit show short, and he was certain this was the last time they could be together.

Her voice was a raspy whisper of "Coming now" before she stiffened and jerked in his arms. He held her close; his grip was probably too tight. But, fuck, he loved touching her.

When she'd quieted, he loosened his hold, aware that he was probably a freak for the way he was with her.

But she smiled at him. "Condom now?"

He thanked all the deities he could remember that she still wanted more, that his last memory of her wouldn't be leaving him hanging.

"I want you inside me, Jonah." He loved the way she said his name. She breathed it, like it was part of her.

He didn't move right away, but he grabbed the back of her neck so she looked at him. "Do you know how much I want to get there?"

Her eyes got big and soft at his growl. She knew it was worse than his bite. But, then again, she liked his bite just fine. "Not enough to get a condom right now?"

To make her point, she rubbed her wet center against his dick, drawing out sounds from both of them. But he wasn't done talking yet. He didn't know why, but he needed her to know just how much she'd affected him in their short time together.

"I'll wake up thinking that I'm going to roll over and see you tomorrow and a bunch of mornings after that." He rubbed one hand down her side, and she buried her head in the crook of his neck. So he spoke into her ear. "When I don't, I'll grab my dick. Because I'll be so hard for you. Just you."

"Will you get yourself off?" she whispered. So, she was on board with the talking.

"I will, but it won't be my big, clumsy hand. It will be yours." She moved her hand back to his cock and rubbed. He sighed.

"What will I do with my hand?"

"That thing you did last night." She added a twist that had him pumping up into her grip.

"What else will I do?" And then she squeezed, and the time for talking was over.

"You'll get a condom and fuck me."

She laughed and scrambled over his shoulder to get to the nightstand. Once she'd rolled it on, he surged up inside her just as she slammed her hips down.

"You want it hard, princess?" Her heat melted over him, soothing him just as surely as she stirred him up inside.

"Yes," she hissed. "I won't break. Fuck me. Fuck me. Fuck me." She punctuated each plea with a slam of her hips into his.

He rolled them over, and elevated her pelvis to get a better angle, so he could rub her clit on every stroke inside, to draw out a long moan. "This what you want? Are you going to miss this?"

Not that he expected answers to his questions, but he wanted them out there. He wanted to know that she was going to think about him when she was all alone. At the same time, he knew she would find someone else. But he couldn't help feeling like this would be wasted on them.

"Yes. Oh my. Fuck. Yes." He wanted to think that she was answering his questions, but she was coming again. Watching her blush all over and yell her pleasure had his orgasm rolling through him. She'd cut him wide open and exposed all the soft bits that he thought he'd killed off over the years.

He didn't know how he'd put himself back together again now.

He withdrew to dispose of the condom, but he wanted to hold onto her just a little longer. "Oh shit."

"What?" Her eyes popped open, but she didn't move from her wrecked-prone position on the bed.

"The condom broke."

She laughed. "That's because your big dick was way too much for it."

"You're not worried?" He was. She didn't know it, didn't need to know it, but this was a big fucking deal for him.

She raised herself up on her elbows and looked at him where he held the destroyed prophylactic in one hand, scrunching up her nose at the sight of so much *him* in his hand. "I told you, it's not the right time of the month. We're both clear on all our tests, so it's fine."

"What if it's not fine?" He hadn't meant to say that. All too well, he knew what could happen when it was not fine.

"We're adults, Jonah." She touched his chest. "Cell phones exist. If it's not fine, I'll call you, and we'll figure it out."

"You'll get rid of it?" He was thinking that there was a baby, when chances were that there was no baby. Having a baby with Carla wouldn't be terrible, and the idea that she wouldn't want to have a baby with him stirred up a shame cocktail in his gut.

"That's not what I'm saying." She touched his arm, rubbed it. He instantly felt better. He hadn't wanted their last interaction to be arguing over an embryo that they weren't even sure existed. Plus, she really shouldn't have his baby. It would be too big and probably break her frame in half. "I'm just saying we'll cross that bridge when—if—we come to it." She sat up and kissed his shoulder. "Get rid of that thing. I want to cuddle while you're still being nice."

He cleaned up the mess in the bathroom before rejoining her in bed, trying to put the broken condom out of his mind but failing. Still, he held her tight, wanting to soak up all of her that he could.

Chapter 14

Six Weeks Later

"So, what are you going to do?" Alana's words didn't register for several seconds. Carla thought of the home pregnancy test she'd taken that had her feeling disembodied. At least she wasn't nauseous. If only she could bottle this feeling of shock and use it to combat the stomach flu that she now knew was morning sickness.

She sank to one of the pink couches in the lobby of the bridal salon where they were waiting to try on bridesmaids' dresses for her sister's wedding.

"We can go to New York the week after the wedding and take care of it." Her sister-in-law-to-be, Maya, chimed in. "No one in the Junior League has to find out."

That snapped Carla out of her fugue state. She didn't fault any woman for her choice, but her heart ached for having a baby. "I don't want to get rid of it."

Both Alana and Maya simply nodded; they kept their faces neutral, waiting for her to let them know how to respond. They'd respect her and support her. They might even be able to stop her parents from disowning or killing her. Unmarried and pregnant was not how the Hernandez family rolled.

Did she want this? She'd wanted a baby so badly that she'd almost married the wrong guy. She'd thought that losing essential parts of herself—her joy, her quirks—was worth it. When Geoff left her, the pain hadn't been about losing him; it had centered on the life she'd sacrificed so much for and still lost.

Her night with Jonah had made her feel like a complete human again. It had shaken up her plans for the future. And she didn't feel awful about it.

Not that Jonah was the right guy, but having his baby was nowhere near a disaster. She found herself almost liking the idea.

She looked up at both the other women and laughed. This whole situation was ridiculous. Waiting to try on her bridesmaid's dress while she had a positive pregnancy test in a plastic bag in her purse. She'd virtually crushed the plastic thing in her fingers when the second line appeared, and she'd carried it with her because she needed her sisters to tell her that it was really real.

She was pregnant.

"When are you going to tell Geoff?" Alana asked. A totally practical question *if* the baby belonged to her ex-fiancé.

"It's not Geoff's baby," Carla said the words quietly.

She hadn't told either Alana or Maya about her one night with Jonah. She'd secreted away her memories and clutched them close since returning from Cuba. And she'd attributed her fatigue and malaise in the past few weeks to a minor bruised heart—kind of like what happened when new trauma was introduced to a healing wound. Although she hadn't regretted having sex with Jonah—still didn't—the whole thing felt bittersweet.

Her time with Jonah had been precious, and she still wanted more. Getting stuck with him had shown her what she could have. She'd thought it had just given her a new target to aim for—a target for how she wanted to feel about someone she could make a commitment to.

And now she'd just made a commitment to be a mother. *Holy fuck. She was going to be someone's parent.*

"Who's your baby daddy?" Maya asked, a twinkle in her eye. Alana slapped Maya in the arm.

"I met him in Cuba."

"A local?"

"No, Tia Lola's boarder." Carla looked down at the test again. "He's a photojournalist. He's probably in Uzbekistan or something right now."

Maya pursed her lips. "So, the perfect candidate for fatherhood then?" Her future sister-in-law had the world's worst father, which might be an understatement. He was in prison for trying to kill her mother.

Jonah would be a better father than that, but by how much? Would he want to be around? Would he want to know that she was pregnant?

He'd given her his number, and she'd promised to let him know if the broken condom had any consequences, but this was a nightmare. She felt swamped by guilt; she'd told him that it wasn't the right time of the month. She'd made a mistake.

"This is my fault, Maya." Carla didn't want to hear Jonah denigrated.

Despite what she'd thought about him at first, he was a good man. He didn't deserve to be saddled with her *and a baby* because she didn't know enough about her own body.

"Excuse me, but did you tie him down and *force* him to sperminate you?" Maya's words were too loud, and Carla wanted to strangle her right now. She could see the headlines: "Jilted, Pregnant Socialite Snaps at Bridal Salon." That would get people talking. Maybe she could get them to focus more on the murder part and less on the pregnant and jilted bit.

"No." She looked around to make sure no one was looking. "And we used condoms."

"Plural condoms?" Alana piped up now, always the lawyer. Now that Alana sensed blood in the water, Carla would have to tell the whole story. She wouldn't have a choice.

"Lola left before the storm hit. So, we were stuck together at the house, and we got bored." Carla hesitated. She still wasn't sure why she didn't want to tell them how she really felt about Jonah, that she cared about him.

"Hernandez?" She was saved when the saleslady came out of the back room. When she saw them, she clapped her hands and turned, daring them not to follow.

Carla got up. She looked at the test again in her purse, just to make sure it was still there and she hadn't dreamed the whole thing. She followed the saleswoman. Alana and Maya followed her. They'd likely been waiting to see if she'd want to call the whole thing off. Carla might be a lot of things these days, but she was for damned sure going to be the best maid of honor there ever was.

They went into a room, all in pink and white, and the saleswoman pushed out a rack of dresses. Carla smoothed her hand over her lower belly. Hopefully the dress still fit. When would she get fat? Would she be fat in a week at the wedding? Then, everyone would know she was knocked up and alone. How embarrassing. This whole thing was mortifying.

And kind of wonderful at the same time.

Maya busked her with her shoulder. "Relax. You're barely pregnant. And you look positively skeletal as usual."

"I haven't been eating much. The idea of food has made me nauseous." Carla found her dress, a blush-pink silk sheath that she had picked out for the whole wedding party. Her older sister didn't care about wedding stuff; she cared about her fiancé, Cole. She was happy for her sister, but something inside her burned with the fear that she would never have what they had. Who wanted to date a single mom?

Alana plopped into one of the chairs. "Are you going to tell him over the phone?"

"I don't know." Carla grabbed her dress and went into one of the curtained alcoves. "It's not really the kind of thing you tell a guy on a satellite phone while he's getting shot at."

"Sheesh. Is his job really that dangerous? Or are you making it sound worse than it really is?" Maya's voice was muffled from the opposite end of the changing area.

Carla really wasn't sure how dangerous his job was on a daily basis. His time in Cuba didn't seem to be that adventurous—other than the tropical storm—but she didn't know him at all really. This was the whole reason why she'd stopped having one-night stands and tried to settle down with someone solid in the first place.

"I can't believe I screwed up like this." Carla felt like she was always screwing up. She shimmied into the dress and looked in the mirror, pleased to see that it fit. In fact, the boob area was a better fit than before she went to Cuba. She came out of the dressing room, and a seamstress swooped in to pin the hips and waist for some final adjustments. "Don't take that in too much."

The seamstress didn't say anything, but her nod was knowing to say the least. Carla needed to fix this mess, and now. She had to tell him, but she also needed to make it clear that she expected nothing. Wanted nothing. Even if that was a lie.

She'd never dreamed of having a baby alone, but she would do that if Jonah didn't want to be involved. Still, there was a big part of her that wanted him in her life.

But trying for a relationship right now would be a horrible idea. Too complicated. Even if a complicated relationship would be much easier to sell to her parents as the reason for their first grandchild.

Much easier than a one-night stand.

* * * *

Jonah's phone rattled against the thrift store coffee table in his apartment, startling him out his action-packed evening of staring at the water-stained ceiling. He'd begged off an invite to a cocktail party Charlie had invited him to. Normally, he'd go and drink the free booze and watch his buddy hit on models. But the idea of a party reminded him so much of Carla that he'd sat there, immobile.

Not that they'd ever been to a party together, but he wondered what it would be like to go with her on his arm. How it would be if she had the brightness and confidence he'd started to glimpse before they both left the island.

He'd never been prone to maudlin thinking, the projection of things that would never be. He'd always been a "here and now" kind of guy. But Carla made him think of a whole lot more than here and now. And he didn't know what to do about it.

He wanted to see her again, even though they lived in different cities—and different worlds. But he wasn't about to ask her to wait around for him while he was getting his ass shot at in some foreign shit hole. And he wasn't going to ask her to leave her family and come to Vietnam or Tokyo at the drop of a hat if he just happened to find a gig there.

Carla's name flashed on the screen and he couldn't help but smile. He hadn't thought that she would call. He felt a stab of guilt that he hadn't called sooner. Had she been waiting for him to make the first move? That seemed like a very Carla thing to do.

As soon as he picked up, she said, "Do you want to go to my sister's wedding with me?"

He spoke the word before thinking about it. "Yes."

"Oh, thank God." Her relief was palpable over the phone line. "Geoff's going to be there, and I don't want to go alone."

He immediately regretted saying yes. She was just going to use him to make her ex jealous. Certainly there were better guys–more local guys—who could do that for her. He also didn't know if he wanted to see Carla in her element. They'd had one night together, but it had meant more to him than it should. Would things even be the same when they weren't stuck together in the same place? Or would they go back to being antagonists? After all, he might be able to fake it at cocktail parties every so often, but he wasn't smooth. He wouldn't impress her ex or her parents because he wasn't a master of the universe, and he never would be.

"I want you there, too." She hesitated. "I want to see you."

Her follow-up words smoothed most of his rancor about being her beard. "Are you sure you want *me* there?" He rubbed a hand over his head. "Isn't this a family thing?"

"Lola is coming." She knew exactly how to twist the knife in. "I know she'll want to see you."

Carla had left the island shortly after the last time they'd had sex. She'd wanted to help with the cleanup from the storm, but *Daddy* had airlifted her ass out of there as soon as possible. Even if he didn't think that Hector Hernandez gave his youngest daughter enough credit, he could see where Carla got her logistical skills. Hector had even had Charlie beat.

So Jonah had time with Lola when she'd returned from her mountain retreat. It took her about five seconds to guess that something had happened between him and Carla while she was gone. She would think it was delightful if they were actually dating. Hell, Jonah would have kind of liked to pretend that Carla belonged with him for a few days.

He didn't think he should go without telling her the truth. That someone would Google him, and she would realize that he wasn't the kind of man who you showed off.

But he couldn't get himself to tell her now. His desire to see her again, to smell her, to touch her was too much to resist.

"Okay. Where and when? What's our cover story?"

Chapter 15

Carla couldn't get her hands to stop shaking while she was waiting for Jonah. Ordinarily, she'd pour herself a glass of wine, but she couldn't do that now. She'd have to wait almost nine months for her next glass of wine. She wondered if she could get her sister to deliver a bottle to the maternity ward or if that would make Child Protective Services show up?

Instead of drinking, she paced.

Carla tried to relax her shoulders and take deep breaths. She could tell him about the baby. She could. He wouldn't get mad at her. Though, if he did, she could handle it.

She looked over at her media stand and the prenatal yoga DVD sitting there. She was shoving it in a drawer when his heavy hand struck the door.

He looked amazing standing on her threshold. Carla had to shove down the desire to pull him in the apartment and push him to the floor so she could mount him. Jonah Kane made her stupid, and he made her forget.

Would it be so bad if he made her forget one more time before she told him about the pregnancy?

Yes, that would make her a bad person. But the way he stared at her—hungry—made her weak.

When she welcomed him into her condo wordlessly, he put down his duffle bag in the hall, shut the door behind him, and pressed her against the wall in the foyer.

His mouth came down on hers, keeping the promise of him as a starving man. His tongue invaded her, and his breaths synched up with her drawing in air. Neither one of them wanted to stop to breathe. He tasted so good, so right to her, right now. She didn't want to stop kissing him, not ever.

His arms around her, he pushed her higher against the wall. She wrapped her legs around his hips, loving the feel of weightlessness, the press of his body against hers. She sifted through his hair with her fingers, loving the sensation even more because it was a memory come to life.

She couldn't stop kissing him now. Remembering the look on his face when he held the remains of that last condom told her that he wouldn't be kissing her again when he heard her news. And he seemed to need this just as much, if not more, than she did. She wanted to give him this before she shattered him.

He burrowed his massive hand up her top, groaning when he found her braless. She cried out when he pinched her nipples. They were crazy tender from the hormones swirling through her system, and the pain was the only thing that could take her out of this moment. "Ouch."

He stopped everything and placed her back on the ground. His lips slick and swollen from the way they'd assaulted each other immediately upon entry. His gaze went soft and roved over her until she caught her breath.

"You're okay."

He couldn't know how loaded that question was. She was safe and healthy. But her mind was kind of a mess. On the one hand, she was happy to see him. Just having him looming over her, concern on his face and the careful way he held her now made her feel so good that she could almost forget what a disaster this was. On the other hand, she was letting him comfort her when he was going to be the one hurting soon.

She opened and closed her mouth several times, hoping that she could just say it. But she couldn't get the image of him walking straight back out the door out of her head. She couldn't get the sounds of the biting words he'd dealt out to her when she'd first arrived in Havana out of her brain.

Tears popped out of her eyes fully formed, stinging her skin, already sensitive from the brush of his beard against her face.

"What's wrong?" He sounded panicked, which somehow resonated as totally masculine on Jonah. "Do you want me to call someone?"

She took one of his hands in both of hers and steered him toward the living room. Looking away from him gave her enough time to stuff her emotions down. Playing hostess was the only thing that came naturally to her at the moment. "Can I get you something to drink? A beer maybe?"

He stopped short behind her. She could feel his body bristling with tension, and his confusion came off of him in waves. Although they didn't know each other that well, she knew that he was not the type of man to smooth over her breakdown in the entryway.

"Turn around, and tell me why you were crying." His words were hard. "Tell me what's wrong."

Carla also knew that he was not the type of man who gave orders. He was conscious that his size was intimidating, and he only used it for good. He didn't have to tell people what to do. They did what he wanted without their even knowing he was telling them. Somehow, his presence steered them.

His words brought her to a halt. She turned to him. "Sit down."

He shook his head. "Not until you tell me what's wrong, princess."

"I'm pregnant."

* * * *

Jonah had known this was a possibility when that condom broke. But, on the plane, he'd allowed himself to push it out of his mind. She would have told him over the phone. *She would have told him over the phone.*

His legs gave out on him and he sat down in the middle of her living room, wedged between her fancy glass coffee table and couch that probably cost more than half a year's rent. He dropped his head between his knees and tried to breathe.

Carla rushed over to him, but she kept her hands poised above him—he could feel her heat—as though she didn't know whether it was okay to touch him. He still wanted her to touch him, but he couldn't get words out.

"It'll be okay." She sounded shaky.

How would this be okay? It wasn't okay the last time, and this would go to shit just like it had back then. Carla was still shaky because of her break up,and now he'd done this to her. What the fuck was wrong with him? Why did he have to be with her one last time? He was a greedy fucking bastard, and he would never learn—taking something good when it was offered to him never turned out well.

During all his adult life, Jonah had never contemplated becoming a father. He didn't know his father, and most of the examples he had growing up were bad. And who knew if Carla wanted him to be this kid's father? He didn't look like anyone's idea of a good dad. He worked all the time in dangerous places. His experience with infants was nonexistent. And he'd seen too many bad things to be able to convince a kid that he could keep her safe.

Jonah was ill equipped at best, probably unfit. His heart pounded, and he couldn't seem to get air into his lungs. The walls of the perfectly decorated condo closed in on him, and he tasted bile at the back of his throat.

He looked up just as she knelt down right in front of him. Immediately, he worried if she should be doing that. Would it hurt the baby? Then, he felt stupid because he didn't know what would hurt a pregnant woman. A woman he had made pregnant.

When he was in a war zone or taking pictures, he was pretty good at forgetting that he had a past. Even before Carla had told him she was pregnant, something about her made it harder to push down, harder to put away. Maybe because she made him feel something. That was why he'd talked to her like he had when she'd first arrived. And this woman, who made him feel…everything…was going to have his baby.

"It's mine." He didn't have to ask the question. She wouldn't lie to him. She wouldn't be like Katie.

Carla nodded. "I'm sorry. I didn't think this would happen. If I had, I would have gotten a Plan B as soon as I got off the plane." She touched him, just barely letting her hands graze the back of his. As soon as she made contact, he let the breath he'd been holding puff out. His entire body deflated, and he stared at her, wondering what they were going to do.

Finally, he got a good look at her. When he'd mauled her in the hallway, he hadn't taken the time to notice that she was pale with dark circles under her eyes. Just looking at her had gotten him so hopped up that he had to feel her mouth against his again. He didn't need her any less now, but she'd changed everything with two damning words.

"What—what do you want to do?" He twined his fingers around her hand, and something warm spread through him, crowding out the cold of Katie's lies.

She squeezed his hands, interlocking her fingers with his. "I'm keeping it." Carla took a deep breath. "I'm not telling you because I want anything. I just—I just thought you'd want to know."

His stomach clenched at her confirmation that she didn't want him in their baby's life. Did he really come off as such a callous fucker that he wouldn't do the right thing when a girl he'd slept with—a woman he'd come to care about told him she was carrying his baby?

Fuck, that was a helluva change from who he had been he was in college. And that hadn't even been his baby.

Right now, he felt like that college kid. He felt like the guy who had used his money for books to buy a cheap ring for a girl who was carrying someone else's baby. The kid he'd been who'd killed his mother with the news that he was going to drop out of college to become a parent. A kid who'd crushed his mother's dream of his degree and a career in the National Football League. At that moment, he was the same disappointment to his town, his family, and himself.

Just then, a big part of him wanted to push Carla away.

The adult he'd become wouldn't let him do it. "What do you need?"

And then she was crying again. So hard that her shoulders shook.

He pulled her close and lay down right there on the floor, holding her while she cried.

Fuck, she was just as confused as he was, and there was nothing he could do to fix this. She'd had her whole life planned out with the loser dickbag accountant. She'd wanted a home and family with that guy, and he'd pushed her away. Carla had come back to life during a few days in Cuba, and now she was crying again.

She was trying to comfort him when everything she'd ever planned for or believed about herself had fallen away. And it was all his fault.

This kind of shit didn't happen in her world. He knew her parents were Catholic. Were they going to expect her to get married? Were they going to expect her to give her baby up if she didn't? Was he lying to himself that this wasn't really like Katie all over again?

He couldn't ask her these questions because it didn't seem like she knew about his past. Probably impossible, but the idea that he would have the opportunity to tell her himself gave him some hope right now. Maybe he could do things right this time.

He wanted to tell her right then, but he rubbed her back until she calmed. He told her that everything would be all right over and over, until he almost believed it himself.

Chapter 16

Carla woke up with her face in Jonah's armpit. Instead of moving, she burrowed in deeper. Maybe her pregnancy hormones were making her crazy, or maybe they'd altered her sense of smell so that the faint hint of her partner's body odor didn't turn her stomach.

Or maybe,= he'd just been so fucking perfect comforting her that she didn't want to puke from his smell. Whatever it was, she was there for it.

The steady breaths he took that moved her whole body told her that he was still asleep. He'd taken a quick trip to China before coming here, and he had to be exhausted from flying halfway across the globe to be with her at her sister's wedding.

She didn't regret inviting him, though. If he was there, then her family would at least know and have one good memory of her baby's father before she made up a breakup story that put him in the best light possible. This was her mistake; she was the family screw-up. So, she would have to deal with the consequences. She didn't want him to have any blowback.

She was not sure what story she could tell that would keep her father and brother from hunting Jonah down with a shotgun, but she would come up with something.

He stirred, and so did everything in her body. Even though they were in one of the most awkward situations ever, it didn't turn off how much she wanted him, how desperate for hot, sweaty fucking he made her.

She turned her head into his chest and pressed her lips to where his heart beat below her. He grumbled, and all of the sudden he was awake. His hardening cock pressed against her ribcage.

"How long did we sleep?" She loved the sound of his voice when he'd just woken up. He sounded like a cranky, old man, and it delighted her. It reminded her of the first day they'd met.

When their kid asked about her dad, she would tell her that he always sounded cranky but never in a bad way.

He shifted underneath her, but she wasn't ready to move yet. She propped her chin on her hands and examined his face. His lips curled into a come-fuck-me smile, and she wanted that. They could talk about what would happen after he left—after she had his baby—later. Right now, she needed to feel their connection. She needed his body to tell her that things were going to be okay—even if they weren't.

"Are you okay?" Although his erection poking into her was telling her that he was on the same page, the concern in his voice said differently. "I'm sorry I didn't call."

"Why didn't you?"

"I didn't think you wanted to hear from me."

"I did."

"Why didn't you contact me? I mean, before you knew about—"

"I didn't want to bother you. I was here, thinking about you nonstop." She rubbed a tiny tear in his T-shirt, right at his collarbone. The cotton was so soft that it was like part of his body. The way this man wore a T-shirt should be outlawed. "I know you have work that's important."

"That's all different now." He scooted her up his body until they were face-to-face. He rucked up his shirt in the process, and his skin felt so amazingly warm that she wanted to burrow in again. She couldn't resist dropping a kiss to his neck. "Don't try to distract me, princess. We have to talk about what we're going to do."

We're. The word was so heavy that it coated her skin with hope. It gave her ideas of having him in her life permanently, of waking up to his cranky voice all of the time. It wasn't fair that she wanted to take him away from the job that he loved, but she couldn't help what she wanted from him. Still, she tried to ignore it, and focus on distracting him from the big talk he wanted to have.

"I don't want to talk." She bit into the skin where his neck and shoulder met, licking him there when his hands tightened on her hips. "And I don't think you do either."

"This is how we got into this." He didn't try to move her, though. Not even when she rolled her hips against him to get some friction.

"I think we're both stressed out by the news, and I think this will help." He sat up and pulled her legs around him so they sat on the floor entwined together.

"You want this now, even after I got you pregnant?" She didn't miss the hint of something—something that didn't sound totally freaked out—in his voice. It sounded like pride. She recognized it as the same thing that hit her brother's voice when he talked about starting a family with Maya, the same glimmer that Cole had when he walked into a room and saw Alana.

She was probably imagining things, but she wasn't inventing the way Jonah was holding her now. "Please." She didn't want to sound like she was begging, she really didn't, but she would set aside her pride for him. She had none when it came to him. That's why she could cry in front of him, fall apart, and act like a mess. She could sob all over him, and he'd still want her—he'd still want to take care of her. "I want you right now."

He grunted and kissed her again. His mouth was salty, and she didn't know if it was her tears or the sweat on his skin. She wrapped her arms around his neck and pulled him so close he couldn't escape her. She should care about whether he wanted to get away, but she didn't.

He rubbed one hand up her bare back and the other down the back of her skirt. She yelped when he clasped one cheek in his hand and squeezed. When he pulled back for just a second, he muttered something like, "Fuck, you're so beautiful, princess."

She smiled against his mouth. "What are you going to do about it?"

He put her away from him then, which made her think that teasing him right now was wrong. She shouldn't be doing that when they were dealing with something so serious. But the look on his face was the opposite of grave; it was get-your-pants-off-right-now sexy. "Bedroom."

They both stood up, and Carla led him to her room. His hand went to her lower back as soon as she was upright. She paused at the threshold, wondering what he thought of where she lived. Where she was going to take care of their infant. She wondered if he was noticing that nothing was baby-proofed.

She wondered all that until he kissed the back of her neck. "What are you going to do now that you've got me here?"

She turned and kissed him on the mouth before he straightened up. She tugged on the bottom of his T-shirt and pulled until it was over his head and she finally got her hands on his bare skin again. He was a wall of man in front of her, so she took a long turn over his body with her eyes.

For his part, he waited, hands clenched at his sides. "Seen enough?"

She smiled up at him. "Never." She thought it was probably too much to say that. He wasn't thinking about forever, certainly not with her. She would just be a footnote in his big, bold life. But, she would never tire of looking at him. She saw something different every time she was with him. He was being careful with her now. Like she was fragile. As breakable as she felt, she wanted to rip away his careful façade and make him give her the hungry lover, the one who had admired her cool head in getting ready for the storm.

She wanted to give him permission to dive in and take her. The need to be claimed pulsed at her core. She needed to let him know. So, she raised her hands overhead. "You haven't seen enough, though, have you?"

He gulped when he must have realized that she wanted him to take off her clothes. "Never."

"What are you waiting for?"

He didn't speak, just pulled off her shirt, and threw it to the side. He ran one finger around one of her nipples, gentle this time. Her whole body shuddered with pleasure. He kept his touch soft as he trailed the same finger down her torso, rubbing the skin right above her pants.

She reached down to undo the button, uncertain whether he could manage to get it through the hole with his thick fingers. And not wanting him to stop touching her that way.

He backed her up to the end of her bed. She pulled down her skirt and underwear, and he dropped to his knees. He kissed each hipbone, and she threw her head back at the feel of his beard and lips against her skin. Her body remembered how much it liked his face buried at the center of her.

"Need you."

He sat her down on the end of the bed and trailed a hand up her body. She felt like he could cup her whole abdomen if he wanted to. Then she realized that he was touching her baby. His face was focused on where his hand lay.

If he didn't want to fuck her because he thought he would hurt the baby—that his size would hurt them—she was going to kill him. "It's fine for the baby."

He barked out a laugh. "I know." He rubbed his thumb against her hipbone. "I just need a minute." He looked up at her face. "Can you give me a minute?"

Why couldn't he have had his minute before they were naked? She'd give him plenty of minutes after he gave her an orgasm. A sound that was a mixture of annoyed and aroused escaped her lips. She flopped back on the bed, intended to give him his fucking minute.

She opened her legs so that he could get to the orgasm giving as soon as the minute was up. He surprised her by laying a kiss on her inner thigh. "You in need, princess?"

Her "yes" came out as a hiss when he ran his tongue up and down the soft skin at her center. She was so sensitive and ready for him that she was ready to come when his tongue brushed her clit.

"You're more sensitive." He did it again, and her back arched off the bed. "Because you're carrying my baby."

"Yes." She heard the same thing in his voice—something like awe and pride—but she couldn't examine it now that he really went to work. He'd been righteously good at eating pussy in Cuba, but this was something else—something that walked the line between filth and reverence.

Her hands bunched up on the duvet, and her feet flexed along his back. He put his whole body into giving her pleasure. His back was sweating, and his muscles flexed. When she felt the tip of his finger at her entrance, she bucked up into it. "I need it now, Jonah. Please, please, please, please."

She felt his groan all over her body as he sank a finger deep inside her. She grabbed his hair and fucked his face and his hand, totally shameless in the face of the mounting release gathered inside her and about to spring out.

"Right there. Yes, please." He got more into it the more she talked, so she kept going. "You're so good. Jonah. So good. I love it when you—"

Her words cut off when her orgasm hit her, as though her brain froze like an old computer. Or like he'd hit the restart button on her insides.

When she finally sagged against the bed and let go of his hair, he knelt back on his calves, pulling all his body heat away from her. She sat up, craving more of him.

The look on his face told her she wasn't going to get any more though. His cock was still making a tent in his jeans, but the serious face was back.

"Jonah, you're not going to hurt me." She gestured at his lap. "It's big, but it's not that big."

He hung his head, shaking it so hard it looked like he was trying to dislodge something troubling from his brain. "It's not that, Carla." He wiped the back of his hand across his mouth, as if he'd just done something tawdry.

Warmth for him wound its way through her chest and pricked the back of her eyes. She'd thought she was all cried out, but what if he felt bad about what had just happened? What if he had been planning to walk out the door when she told him, and instead she'd practically forced him to go down on her? Maybe it really was a pity orgasm this time?

"What is it? We don't have to do that again. We don't have to do anything. Just tell me what's wrong."

He met her eyes then. His face was hard, jaw clenched. But his eyes—they were soft. "This is not the first time I've been in this situation."

* * * *

Carla's mouth gaped open. Jonah sat there and watched while she started several sentences. He didn't know how to tell her the truth in a way that wouldn't make her recoil from him. She'd either feel sorry for him or she would think he was the one at fault, and he really couldn't take that.

"You have a child?"

"No."

"Then one of your exes had a miscarriage."

"Not exactly."

She scooted to the end to of the bed, and curled up in a ball, staring him down. He recognized that look. It reminded him of Lola when she got her mind on something.

Jonah stood up and grabbed a blanket off a plush, grey chair in the corner of the room. Carla's space was classy and neutral. It didn't really fit her. Seemed like an empty-headed debutante lived there. Now that he knew her better, that wasn't who she was at all.

"You didn't know?" He was shocked she hadn't looked him up the second she'd gotten back. Maybe their time together hadn't impacted her as much after all.

"I didn't want to be that obsessive girl. I didn't allow myself to look you up."

He smiled at her then, flattered. "You were obsessed?"

She rolled her eyes. "Yes, you're a very satisfying lover." After he wrapped her in a blanket and sat next to her, she said, "You're freaking me out. Just tell me."

"I played football in college." It seemed best to start at the beginning.

"And?" She motioned for him to proceed. She was probably right. He should just say everything in one go. A rush of relief flowed through his chest.

"I've been this big since I was a sophomore in high school. Well, this tall. So, my mom wanted me to play football. We didn't have a lot of money, and she thought it could help me get a college education." He remembered how proud his mother had been when recruiters started showing up at his games.

"So you were good?" A faint smile touched her lips, and he wanted to grab the hand she had perched on the bed right next to his.

"Yeah, I was good. I was an inside linebacker, and there were talks of me winning the Heisman my junior year. That doesn't happen. Usually, it's a quarterback." She looked impressed by that, and it only made shame spread through his body. "My best friend on the team was a quarterback, and he was on the short list, too."

"Did it ruin your friendship?" Her eyes narrowed. "I don't see what this has to do with getting someone pregnant."

"Our school was Catholic—super conservative—and they had rules. You're not supposed to have premarital sex."

Carla guffawed, same as most people did when they heard about a college trying to stop nineteen-year-olds from boning. "That's actually ridiculous."

"Yeah, but my mom was religious—I was religious—back then."

"You're not now, right?" She ran one finger across his palm, and he finally gave himself permission to grab her hand. "I didn't force you into compromising on your beliefs or anything?"

"No, but, back then, I would do anything but intercourse. A loophole if you will."

"No wonder you're so good at eating pussy." She gave him a teasing half-smile.

He felt his skin heat. Maybe she was right. Or maybe it was just her that made him want to make everything good for her.

"My best friend, he was a golden boy, and my girlfriend—"

"Your girlfriend cheated on you with your best friend?" The fury in Carla's words was somehow calming to him.

"Not exactly. We, um, we had a threesome. And he had sex with her. I was fine with it." He rubbed a hand across his face. "Or, at least, I thought I was."

"Did you want him to touch you in your no-no place? Did he?" Her sarcasm wasn't helping. He supposed, outside of that environment, where he and his teammates were under a microscope from the university, from reporters, it wouldn't be such a big deal. He also came from a small town; his mother's hopes were so pinned on him.

"I felt angry about it afterward. I felt guilty, and I pushed Katie away."

"I still don't see what it has to do with you and me." She wrapped the blanket around her like a sarong and stood up. The fact that he was talking about the period in his life that he wanted most to forget wasn't stopping him from admiring the way the blanket rested between her breasts. He wanted to rip it off and forget all about this, but he needed to be completely honest with her.

"Katie got pregnant. And, because I was her boyfriend, everyone assumed the baby was mine."

"Did you get kicked out of school?"

He shook his head. He'd almost wished he had been kicked out quietly. Then, his family name wouldn't have been dragged through the mud. His mother wouldn't have gotten so stressed out. She wouldn't have had a stroke and died.

"No, we had to go to religious counseling."

"Why did you lie for her?"

Katie had begged him not to tell the dean that the baby wasn't his. She had wanted to get an abortion, but he'd called her names and told her she was ruining his life. Thought he was a hero for facing the consequences of his actions. After all, he'd let it happen. The threesome had been hot, which added a whole different dimension of shame in his mind.

"I cared about her, and her dad was an important donor." Carla was pacing now. "I bought a ring and asked her to marry me."

"You didn't want to marry her." Carla knew what he was trying to say without him having to say it.

"No, and my best friend didn't want anything to do with the baby—or me—after he found out." Tim had actually laughed at him when he'd told him about the pregnancy. He'd called Katie a stupid slut and told Jonah to dump her ass. "Tim and Katie both came from money. Their parents could bail them out of problems with the university. And Tim—he was going to get a fat NFL contract either way."

"That would have helped your mom." Carla's tone was soft, understanding. He wanted to curl his body around hers and never leave this room.

"And then Katie—" Carla was so understanding that he wanted to tell her the worst part—the part that made leaving school without a degree, losing out on the NFL, the humiliation pale in comparison. "She killed herself...because of what Tim said...and what I said." The thought of it—all these years later—made him nauseous.

"After that, I quit the team. Quit school. I couldn't face any more of the interviews or the articles about how I was brave for carrying on in the face of Katie's death. And then my mom—"

Carla stayed silent, and he couldn't look at her. He knew she was probably processing everything, thinking of a way to ask him to leave. He'd done this whole accidental pregnancy thing before, and he'd fucked it up. He couldn't do this.

The only person who knew the whole story was a therapist he saw last year when he'd returned from Aleppo. All the things he'd seen had messed up his head so severely that he knew he needed to talk to someone before he broke down. He hadn't wanted to get out of bed, but he couldn't sleep because of the gruesome images that attacked him every time he slept. The shrink had tried to convince him that Katie killing herself wasn't his fault. She obviously had been dealing with depression before she got pregnant. Jonah regretted that he hadn't supported her in getting help—he regretted the things he'd said to her when they found out about the pregnancy. Nothing would take that away, and nothing could make him forgive himself for that.

"Fuck that!" Her exclamation snapped him out of his self-pitying talk.

"You are not responsible for what she did. You're not responsible for your shitty ex-best friend. You were responsible for you, and you made some mistakes. But, it was a weird, fucked-up situation. And you did your best to make it better. You were going to marry her, even though you weren't sure you wanted to end up with her, just to make sure she didn't get kicked out of school."

"But the news stories were awful. When they found the note saying it was actually Tim's baby, the reporters said that Katie had only ever been my beard, and that Tim and I were lovers."

"Jesus. Who are these people?"

"The football team at my school is like a religion for people. And there are always people wanting to take it down."

"But you were kids. Barely adults. And who cares if you guys were gay?"

"The school. They cared about image." As soon as the first stories broke, Jonah had fallen off the Heisman short list. Coach hadn't reduced his playing time, but his performance had suffered. Eventually, he'd been benched. "And my mom, she was devastated. She had a stroke when she found out I quit school."

"You didn't kill your mother. She wanted the best for you, and the school screwed you over."

"Yeah?"

"Another thing that's not your fault." She caressed his face, and looked like an avenging angel with her sex hair and swollen lips. "Did you ever talk to anyone about this?"

"Not for a long time. No one knew."

"Not even Charlie? You two seem close."

"He doesn't know the whole story. Not what I did."

"I think you have this all twisted up in your head, and you've made everything your fault when it isn't. What did you do that was so bad, really? You experimented sexually, making sure your girlfriend got the kind of sex she wanted with someone you both trusted." She pointed at her own abdomen. "And broken condoms happen."

"Yeah, but Katie died. My mom died."

"You're still here, Jonah. And I'm here. And our baby is going to be here."

Carla's belief in him gave him hope, made his heart beat faster, but he couldn't let himself forget that she didn't want him around either. She just wanted him to come to the wedding with her so she wouldn't have to face her ex alone. He was just a sperm donor in this situation. She might like to fuck him, but he was not going to be around to father their baby.

Still, he didn't stop Carla when she cupped his face and kissed him on the mouth. He didn't stop her when she dropped the blanket and went to her knees between his legs. He didn't bother to correct her when she kissed his stomach after saying he was a good man, making every ounce of blood in is body drain into his cock.

He only stopped her when she put her hand over his cock and squeezed. "What are you doing?"

She looked at him, a determined set to her jaw. "I understand that this is a big deal in your life. It's embarrassing, and you think it makes you damaged goods." She grabbed the hand he had clenched on his knee, and he let her. "But you were a kid from a small town. You got in over your head with a girl and with a friend you couldn't trust. You tried to take responsibility, and things didn't work out." Then she kissed his palm. Her acceptance of him made him so uncomfortable that he wanted to pull away. He tried, but she held tightly onto him. "We're adults now, and we have choices. I'm stronger than her. I know it doesn't seem like it, but I'm not going anywhere."

"I don't want to go anywhere, either." He'd been thinking that she was going to send him on his way as soon as he told her the truth. Hearing her defending him—way too late to change anything, of course—straightened out something in his brain. Maybe this was his chance to correct his mistakes and move on.

"You don't have to go anywhere. I want you here." He pulled her up to kiss her then, dragging her with him as he lay down on the bed. She gave him reassurance with her kiss that he could never have gotten from words. She felt so good to him, like a dream with all her creamy skin lined up against his body. She rolled and pressed against him, mimicking fucking.

When she sat up, straddling his belly, he felt her wet and ready against him. Her eyes still held fire, but with lust this time. "You didn't just say all that so you could get back in my pants, did you?"

He shouldn't have said that because the expression on her face darkened, and she leaned over until her face was kissing distance from his. She held him down, though, so he couldn't get at her mouth and soothe his words away with actions.

"This is a weird situation, and now that I know all this, a weird situation is the last thing either of us need." She dropped a kiss on his cheek that felt almost playful. "But our weird situation isn't going anywhere." She grabbed his cock through his jeans, and he bucked up into her hand. "So, we might as well give into it."

Chapter 17

Carla wanted Jonah so much, even more after hearing what he had been through. She hated everyone involved in that terrible situation that had hurt him. She even hated Katie for putting so much of her pain on Jonah before taking her own life.

The only way she could make him believe that she wanted him here and that her getting pregnant by accident wasn't the end of the world was to show him that she was okay and that she needed him.

She rubbed him slowly, firmly, and she could see the strain on his face. "Fuck, Carla. You're going to kill me."

"I hope not. I have quite a bit of use for you."

Finally, that got his mouth to curve into half a smile. Right before he rolled them both over and pinned her body open with his hips. She took the opportunity to pull the buttons on his jeans loose. He grunted when his cock got some freedom.

"If I was going to die, that would be the way I wanted to go."

Carla wanted him to stop talking about death right about now. It reminded her that he had a dangerous job. The kind of job that someone with no one waiting for him at home would take without a second thought. Not the kind of job that someone with a family had.

But she had to put those kinds of thoughts out of her mind. This was about comforting him, giving him what he needed—showing him that she was right there for him.

She hooked her toes into the waistband of his jeans and jerked them down. He kicked them the rest of the way off while got to work on his boxers. She felt like he'd been keeping her waiting for days instead of the few hours since he got here. In reality, she'd been waiting since the last time, for seven weeks.

Once they were both naked, he held himself off of her. His cock nudged her thigh and she rolled up into his body, hoping he'd put her out of her misery. But he just stared at her like she was something wonderful and precious to him. Now that she knew that he expected to lose anyone who was important to him, she couldn't handle him looking at her like that. As though she was going to evaporate if he didn't hold her tight.

She kissed his mouth, pulling him closer to her with her hands and then roaming them over his broad shoulders. Her hands traveled down his sides over the muscle, sinew, and bone that made his weight against her body so deliciously solid.

She got so lost in feeling him that if she hadn't been waiting so long—if she didn't feel so empty without him inside her—she'd forget all about sex and kiss him for hours and days. But she needed him, and he must have heard her soft whimpers against his lips because his cock was at her entrance, just lingering there.

"I haven't been with anyone." His words were a whisper.

"I haven't either." He rubbed the head across her clit. She was so close she was ready to pant and beg. "Please, please, please."

"You're so greedy, but not like I first thought when we met. I like it that you're greedy for my cock." He pressed in, just a little, but not enough. She grabbed his ass to try to push him fully inside her, but he resisted, chuckling. "I love it when you make that little frustrated noise. Like you're scared you're not going to get what you want. I always want to give you everything you need, princess. But you have to tell me."

Tell him what? He couldn't possibly expect her to put words together when he was torturing her. Just some of him was torture. She wanted all of it, so hard and big that she *would* get scared for a second. So deep inside her that her eyes would water.

"C'mon, princess. Say the words so I can give you what you need."

She made another frustrated whine and tried to pull him in again. "Please, Jonah. Come inside. I need you."

The muscles along the back of his body shuddered against her hand, and he sank into her. He wasn't too big for her, but he split her open with a million little explosions as the length of him caressed her and as the skin at the base of his cock stroked her clit every time he hit bottom.

She wanted to cry, but only because it felt so good. So delicious. "How do you have this much control?" Her breath was panty, but she needed to know.

He was caught off guard by her question, slowing. When she tried to pull him again, he levered up and put her hands over her head. "I'm used to not giving in. I did that for a long time."

"But I want you now." She pouted because he still hadn't started up again. He examined her, trailing the hand that wasn't restraining her over her breasts, ribs, and her belly before finding her clit with his thumb.

"Do I ever not give you what you need?" He rubbed, making a rhythm that had her back to that begging place again.

"You do. You do."

"Then trust me."

"I trust you. I do." She trusted him totally. He'd always been so careful with her. Despite anything that might be in his past, despite the fact that they had wildly different personalities, she knew in her bones that he would keep her safe. There was something primal about the combination of his size and their chemistry. It transformed something that shouldn't work into something that felt like home. It should be terrifying, but she wanted to get closer to the flames threatening to overtake them. She wanted to be bowled over by the force of it.

His hand stilled, and she whined again. She hated that he had this much control over her body, but she knew he needed that right now. She knew him better than she ought to after spending a couple of days with him.

"Trust me to give you what you need." Finally, he sank back inside her and fucked her like he intended to finish it.

"Yes, Jonah. Yes."

"I love hearing you say my name, princess."

She didn't even flinch when he used the l-word. They weren't in love; it was too soon for that. Saying she was in love with him would be even crazier that trying to make a relationship with the guy who'd knocked her up work. A guy who knocked her up who could die any time he left home to go to work. But realistic worries about their future had no place right now when he was driving them both into an apocalyptic orgasm—one that could change the landscape of the earth.

He lost control and pumped faster and harder. Every atom inside her curled up and burst out, frying half her brain cells until she felt drunk and drowsy. As soon as she clenched his cock tight and cried out, he reared back and pressed into her one last time. She felt him come inside her for the second time, and she didn't have words for how good that felt.

Before he rolled off of her, he kissed her. He thanked her, and she started to cry.

Everything in her chest warmed and softened. She wanted to hold him so tight, forever. She wanted him so much it ached in her. When he held her close and kissed the back of her neck, she wondered if she could keep him here.

Chapter 18

Jonah hadn't let anyone pick out his clothes since he was about six. Even then, his mother hadn't had a lot to choose from, so her picking out his clothes was largely a brief assessment of what was clean.

Carla fussing over his suit was different. He hadn't had a woman fuss over him in so long it made it feel like the clothes didn't actually fit, when they did. He pulled at the cuffs of the shirt she'd told him to wear to the rehearsal dinner.

"Stop fidgeting. You look great."

"I don't see why we had to go shopping." He didn't like that the clothes he'd brought with him hadn't been good enough for her.

"I never see a reason *not* to go shopping." She giggled as she walked out into the hallway of her condo building. "Geoff hated when I shopped."

Jonah gritted his teeth at the mention of her ex-fiancé. "Is he going to be there tonight?"

They made it to the elevator, and he put his hand on her lower back. As usual, touching her calmed down his jumping nerves. He hadn't met anyone's family since Katie. Considering how that ended, he wasn't sure what to expect.

"You need to relax." She looked up at him, her eyes dancing. Somehow, even though he'd kept her up most of the night—proving her wrong about his control when it came to her—she looked less tired than she had when he'd arrived at her condo the day before. "My parents are going to like you."

"You think?" He'd done research on the Hernandez family while Carla was in the shower that morning. There was plenty of information about them in the local press, and Carla's father had had a few profiles done on him on finance-focused sites and blogs. Hector Hernandez had been a major player in Miami; people on Wall Street paid attention to what his firm was doing. He'd built the company from the ground up, and though he was retired, Jonah couldn't imagine that he was less intimidating.

"Well, my mother's going to like you. My dad will probably tell you to cut your hair."

"Why didn't you tell me that before?" Jonah took his hands off of her and tightened his ponytail. "I would have cut it off instead of doing all that shopping today."

Carla turned to him, mischief on her face. "I like grabbing onto it while you're giving me head." She said it like she would say that the sky was blue. "So no cutting the hair. I like the hair." She grabbed his arm. "You're keeping the hair."

"Just don't tell your parents why you like it."

"Ha! My mom will probably guess because my parents are disgustingly in love after thirty-five years."

Jonah had to respect that. His family had been broken before he was born. His mother had chalked up her affair with his father as a huge mistake. Sometimes, growing up, *he* felt like a mistake. His mother had worried so much about him, pinned so many hopes on him, that the responsibility had felt crushing. It had turned out that she was right to be worried.

He'd lost his religion after his mother died, but maybe he could have faith in Carla. Her parents were a good example, so maybe she knew how to do this. Maybe he could trust her to show him how to be good enough for her.

"Stop moping. There's going to be food there. And beer. It's going to be fine." She patted his arm as the elevator doors opened to the parking garage. She walked ahead of him, and he got a full impression of what her dress looked like from behind. It was long and black with a sheen to it that emphasized her curves. She clearly wasn't wearing a bra because it plunged down to the base of her spine.

Later, when they were alone, he would lick his way down her back before removing the dress. Fuck, maybe he would take her while she was still wearing it.

When she stopped at a convertible that looked like a toy, he sighed. How was he ever going to fit in that tiny car? He would look like an idiot getting in and out of it.

"We're driving this?"

Carla unlocked the glorified matchbox with a key fob. "I know I'm going to have to give this up, just like I've given up alcohol and soft cheese, but I'm going to drive this baby until our baby comes."

"You're not even going to let me drive it?"

"No. No one gets to drive my car. I was engaged, and Geoff never even got to drive my car."

Her mentioning him twice in the same conversation made him want to stomp his feet and refuse to go. He hated the guy for hurting her, and he hated that the guy was still around.

Everything in him wanted to find the guy at the wedding tomorrow and beat his face in. But, if he hadn't done the dumbest thing in the world and broken up with Carla, they might never have met. And, even if they had met, he would have had to live with the fact that she was married to an idiot. Because he would have wanted Carla no matter who she was with.

He let out the breath he'd been holding since she told him about Geoff and the car, and he wedged himself inside the tiny vehicle. His knees weren't all the way up to his chest, but they were close. Even itty-bitty Carla was going to have to give up this car before the baby came. Her belly would be too big to drive it in a few months.

Would they have to buy a minivan? The thought of it made sweat break out on the back of his neck. He was going to ruin the shirt that Carla had made him buy.

"What are you thinking about?" Carla revved the engine before peeling out of the garage. "Your thoughts are loud."

"Minivans."

"Ew." She scrunched up her face and changed lanes. "Why would you think about those?"

"Don't parents drive minivans?" He really had no idea what he was doing. They couldn't even have a conversation about a car.

"I was thinking an SUV."

"A big one." She and the baby would be safe.

She patted his knee before shifting gears. "Yeah, we'll find one you fit inside."

* * * *

Carla didn't like how nervous Jonah was. Her father would sense it and pounce on any weakness. She wouldn't be surprised if her father had a full dossier on Jonah—information including what he'd told her yesterday.

Even if she had looked him up after returning to Miami, it wouldn't have changed what happened between them or how she felt about it. He still gave her a flippy-fluttery feeling in her stomach every time he looked at her.

She was still proud to have him on her arm.

By the time they pulled up to the church, he'd calmed down. She could feel it. Her parents and siblings were waiting in the vestibule when they walked in.

Alana, Maya, and Carla's mother all sort of gaped at Jonah. Her brother, Javi, puffed up his chest. Cole smiled, but he grabbed onto Alana's hip a little tighter. Carla didn't care how they reacted to Jonah.

She looked to her father.

Hector Hernandez was an imposing man. He'd terrified most people in the business world. She'd bet he could make a grown man pee his pants with one glare. Her father's eyes narrowed as he assessed Jonah.

Best-case scenario, Hector would nod and then ignore her date for the rest of the night. That's what he'd done with Geoff—and he worked for him. Worst case, he would pull Jonah aside and threaten to destroy his career or kill him. And, given what she now knew about Jonah's past, Carla guessed it would be the latter.

Carla's mother broke the standoff. "You must be Jonah." She walked over and extended her hand. "I'm Molly Hernandez." Her mother's broad smile told her that everything would be okay and that she approved. Even if her father went shotgun wedding on them, her mom would have her back.

"It's a pleasure to meet you, Mrs. Hernandez."

"It's Molly. Mrs. Hernandez was my mother-in-law, and she was a nightmare of a woman."

Carla rolled her eyes. Her family did not have company manners. Not ever. She should have warned Jonah. "Mom…"

Her mother turned to her. "You haven't briefed him on the Hernandez family basics?"

They'd actually been busy being shell-shocked about becoming parents, but she wasn't about to tell her mother that. That would come after Jonah left, and she had to explain that they just didn't know each other well enough to make a go of it. "No, he just got here yesterday, and we've been catching up."

"Carla told me that you helped her get through the storm." Her mother's words made Carla choke on her own spit.

Luckily, Maya walked over and offered her a water bottle with an arched eyebrow. "You okay?" Carla wasn't sure if she was asking her or Jonah. As the newest member of the clan, Maya was the one most recently familiar with their father's propensity toward being an asshole. "I'm Maya Pascual, Javier's fiancée."

Maya sounded surprised to be saying those words. Carla checked for Javier, and he looked as though he was going to burst from hearing them. They had a long, rocky road to being together. Javi had married someone else before realizing that his heart belonged to his longtime friend. Carla couldn't be happier to have Maya as her new sister.

Cole and Alana walked over next. "This is Jonah?" Carla could tell that Alana had a lot she wanted to say—much more that she wanted to ask. She probably wanted all the gritty details. Even though she had more than she could handle, she would demand the information as payback for all the times that Carla had butted into her business when she first got together with Cole.

Back then, Carla thought she knew everything because she'd managed to get herself engaged. Like it was some sort of achievement. She'd been stupid. Particularly so because she'd almost gotten in the way of true love.

"Where's the priest?" Her father ignored Jonah, which came as a relief to Carla, but she felt Jonah tense while standing next to her. "Don't we donate enough to the church to merit him showing up on time?"

"Hector, you've got to relax. You're going to give yourself a heart attack." Maya was the only person, other than Carla's mother, who gave her father rashers of shit. Everyone laughed at it now, but before it had driven a wedge between Javi and their father.

Her father wasn't a modern man, not at all. He looked young for his age, but he was old-school. He believed in honoring one's parents, and the worst thing she could do in his eyes was bring shame to the family. As far as he knew, both his girls were still virgins. He pretended he didn't know that Cole and Alana had been living together for almost two years. Carla thought he might have been okay with Geoff because he didn't see him as a threat to his baby girl's virtue.

Hector walked off to find the rectory and probably read the priest the riot act about timeliness. Carla didn't pity the man. She'd been on the receiving end of that lecture often enough.

"So, Daddy's in a good mood, then?" Carla's question made everyone laugh. Jonah put his hand on her lower back, and she reached back and grasped his fingers.

Chapter 19

Jonah hadn't been back inside of a church since college. Every home game, the whole team had gone to mass in the basilica. Then, they'd paraded to the stadium cheered by fans who'd traveled from all over the world to see them play.

He'd always relished the time inside the church before they had to face the crowds—people who adored the idea of them as gladiators. The quiet had soothed him enough to play well. He'd never been comfortable with the press attention, and he'd been labeled as difficult. Just one of many reasons that reporter had written the first story about him, Tim, and Katie.

Now, in this church, he didn't feel safe or at home. He felt like he was walking an endless gauntlet. Except, this time the fans weren't adoring.

He sat in the back pew, hoping to avoid an interrogation from Carla's father. Although he outsized Hector by a few inches and fifty pounds of muscle, his girl's father had pure hatred on his side. Jonah had sensed it from the get-go. Jonah had less fear when it came to running across roadside explosives or suicide bombers than he did about running across Carla's dad in a dark alley.

Part of him respected the man for wanting to protect her. Jonah couldn't forget that Carla had had an acute broken heart when they'd met. She hadn't been leaving the house, and she'd withdrawn from her busy social life. Watching her with her sister, her mom, and Maya had him wondering if she was in pain now. It had seemed like the pregnancy had displaced the breakup as her major source of anxiety, but what if it was just adding to it? After all, she'd only invited him here so she wouldn't be without a date, not because he was really someone she wanted to spend her life with.

Until she'd opened the door to her apartment, he hadn't known that he'd been willing to change his life to be with Carla. Before she'd told him about the baby, he'd known he wanted Carla, not that he wanted her forever. It should have scared him, but he felt relieved. All of it was so monumental that he couldn't believe he wasn't terrified. But he wasn't. He was only scared that she wouldn't want him just as much.

She probably wasn't having the same yearning at all. He felt so *stupid* wanting to be up there with her. As more than her date. He wanted to belong to her in the same way that Cole belonged to Alana. The man looked at Carla's sister like she was the sun. He wanted to be able to claim Carla the way that Javi claimed Maya—with some words whispered in her ear that made a filthy smile cross her face.

He wanted to be doing for his and Carla's kid what Hector and Molly were doing for theirs. And it made no sense. He and Carla barely knew each other. They'd had two nights together, and insane chemistry, but they didn't know all the annoying things about each other. She might know about his worst thing, but he didn't know about all her best things. He wanted that, but could he really afford to stick around long enough to find out? Wouldn't there be another job? Wouldn't she get sick of waiting for him? Would she tire of how hard it was for him to open up to her?

But watching Cole and Alana practice for their big day had him wanting to try for everything he'd never known he'd wanted with Carla.

Jonah was an aching, confused mess by the time they made it to the restaurant. Everyone talked a lot, so he didn't have to say much at all. He laughed at Alana's stories about her little sister; he had a feeling it was some kind of payback.

And Cole, bless him, made sure his beer stayed full. Once he'd made small talk with the guy, he immediately liked him. Cole told him that he'd been a Navy SEAL and they got to bonding over some of the shittiest posts in the Middle East.

"Shouldn't you be the nervous one, man? You're the one getting married tomorrow." Jonah was grateful that Cole was so welcoming, but giving a family orientation to his sister-in-law's date would be the last thing on his mind if he was in Cole's position.

"Ha. The last thing I have to be nervous about is getting married." Cole took a swig of beer and winked at him. "But I was the new guy once, and it's not easy to integrate oneself into this family without getting swallowed up whole."

"It seems like you belong well enough now." Cole even seemed natural around Hector, which floored Jonah.

"You'll get there. At least no one took a swing at you."

"Hector hit you?" Jonah wasn't sure he could keep himself from hitting back if Hector came after him.

"Nah, it was Javier." Javier looked up from his food after hearing his name. He pointed at his own face with two fingers and then at Cole, the international symbol for "I'm watching you."

"Why'd he hit you? I thought you guys were friends."

"Yep. We were. Such good friends that he knew enough to know that he didn't want me anywhere near his sister."

"You guys worked it out, though."

"Yeah." He pointed at Javi. "I let him beat me to a bloody pulp, then I slunk out of town, realized I was an asshole, and came back and got my girl."

They both looked over at Alana, who had her head bent toward Carla. They had been talking almost nonstop since they'd gotten to the restaurant, and Carla needed to eat. He was a split second from getting up and trying to feed her when Cole whistled. "Any idea what's going on there?"

Jonah had plenty of ideas. Alana was probably trying to talk Carla out of being with him, not that he could really blame her. But it didn't change the fact that he was here, and he'd be here for as long as Carla wanted him around. "No idea. Probably dresses or some shit."

"No, they'd be happy about dresses. I'm pretty sure they're talking about you."

Fuck. His heart sank.

Once they were done eating, Cole pointed out toward the patio of the restaurant. "Javier and I are going to smoke cigars. Even if you don't smoke, you're going to come with us. It's really for your safety." Cole laid a hand on his chest. "I wouldn't be able to live with myself if I left you alone with Hector."

Jonah nodded. He'd smoke cigars until his lungs fell out to avoid a confrontation with Hector.

Javier had the patio bartender pouring scotch when they joined him. Three of them. When he turned around to hand Jonah his drink, he had a wolfish smile on his face that made Jonah nervous.

"Okay. Here's the deal." Javier handed him the drink. "You hurt my baby sister, I disembowel you. I know you've got about thirty pounds on me, but ask this one." He pointed at Cole. "I pack a punch."

"I'm not going to hurt Carla." He was going to try his best not to hurt Carla or their kid.

"Okay then." Javier raised his glass and nodded. "*Salud.*"

They all took drinks. Javier and Cole drained their glasses, but Jonah sipped. He didn't want to get drunk; he had a feeling he'd need to be quick on his feet when Hector finally cornered him.

"Drink up," Cole said. "Hector called me a pansy when I took ten minutes to finish a scotch at Christmas."

"Nah, he called you a pansy because he was telling the story about Carla's engagement party."

Jonah didn't want these guys to know that Carla's prior engagement bothered him. He didn't want to show that he had more than casual feelings for their sister. But, he couldn't help his curiosity. "What happened?"

Javier and Cole shared a look, and then Cole said, "Carla and Geoff were fighting, and it was getting bad. Poor idiot never could do anything right." Cole motioned the bartender for a refill. "Anyway, they were making a scene, so I did some karaoke."

"He's not a good singer." Javier took Jonah's glass and got them both refills. So much for not getting drunk. "And by that I mean he's maybe the worst singer to try to sing ever."

Cole punched Javier in the arm. "I'm no Bobby Brown, but at least I have moves. And she appreciated the gesture enough to take me back. So that's all that matters."

"You singing to her at the wedding tomorrow?" Jonah thought it might be nice.

Cole's eyes got big, and Javier rolled his.

"That'd be so romantic. I should do it." The alcohol had clearly started to kick in.

"If you do that, she'll get the marriage annulled." Javier was still seeing reason. Or Jonah thought so at least before he just motioned the bartender to hand him the rest of the bottle of scotch.

"We shouldn't drink that." Jonah hesitated, and both the other men raised their eyebrows.

"My dad's coming out here with cigars and a mean look on his face." All three of them walked over to a grouping of chairs and couches. Cole and Javier sat on the couch, which left him one of the chairs. So, he'd be facing down Hector. And Carla's brother and brother-in-law would be spectators.

"Neither of you care about spending all my money." Hector pointed at Cole and Javier. He seemed very concerned about how much this wedding cost. Jonah wondered if he would demand to see his finances when he found out about the baby and how serious Jonah was becoming about Carla. He did okay, had been good about saving money. He would have been in a much better position had he made it to the NFL, but he was flush.

"We've been kicking ass at making you even more money," Javier said. "And all you have to do is walk around the house and drive Mom nutters."

"We'll pay you for the scotch, Hector," Cole said, obviously still at the stage where he wanted to mollify Hector.

Hector handed Javier and Cole a cigar before he offered one to Jonah. Jonah had the feeling that this was a test. If he said no to the cigar, he would be failing some sort of contest of manliness.

He took it, and Hector nodded at him. "So, Jonah Kane, I've been looking into your past."

Jonah's stomach dropped, but he lit the end of the cigar and puffed anyway. He wouldn't show weakness. Carla believed in him, and that had to be enough.

"Dad." Javier's voice had a warning tone.

"Carla's my little girl." Hector waved off his son. "I am entitled to keep her safe. She doesn't make the best decisions for herself."

Jonah wanted to fight him then. Carla had chosen Geoff in the first place to get her father's approval. Blaming her for that and characterizing her as flighty now was unfair. She didn't deserve it.

"I'm not a bad decision." He said it because Carla needed defending right now, not because he actually believed he was right for her.

Hector took a puff of his cigar and blew out circles of smoke. With the scotch in his hand and the halo of smoke, he looked like an old-school gangster. "We'll see about that." He took a swig of scotch; Jonah knew Hector wasn't done with him yet. "Just don't get her pregnant and abandon her."

Jonah didn't know how he stopped himself from choking on the sip he'd just taken of his drink. If Hector only knew the truth, he doubted he'd still be standing—or breathing.

"You okay, man?" Cole asked him. "If you're not used to them, these Montecristos are pretty killer."

Cole's question gave Jonah a chance to catch his breath. "Tasty, though."

Chapter 20

Carla didn't know what her father said to Jonah. Whatever it was sent him straight to the bottom of a bottle of scotch. Although, maybe Cole and Javi had something to do with that. She was glad to see that her brother and brother-in-law were welcoming of him. In fact, they were nicer to Jonah than they had been to Geoff at first. But Carla guessed that Jonah was more cut from the same cloth. The prove-I'm-a-man's-man-by-drinking-all-the-scotch cloth.

Still, she did not appreciate having to steer him back to the car. And the smell of liquor and cigar smoke did nothing for the nausea that still came and went throughout the day.

Carla also didn't appreciate seeing her ex-fiancé standing behind the boot of her car. *How did she ever convince herself that she* wanted *this guy?* Looking at him now, she could never imagine sharing a bed with him again. It wasn't that he was ugly; it was that standing next to Jonah—even though she was deeply irritated by his getting hammered with her dad—made her feelings about Geoff crystal clear. She had nothing for him anymore except mild regret. Regret that she'd wasted years on a dweeb who thought all she had to offer was a pedigree and housekeeping skills.

"Geoff, what the fuck are you doing here?"

Jonah stood up ramrod straight for the first time in hours and pointed at Geoff. "This motherfucker?"

"Your new boyfriend is charming, *dear.*"

Carla had always hated that endearment; it sounded like fingernails on a chalkboard. When Jonah had started calling her princess, she'd thought it was the same kind of annoyance, but this was different. Every time she heard Jonah say that word, in that husky sex-crazed voice of his, she felt cherished. Geoff was just condescending to her when he called her dear.

"I don't see how that's any of your business." Carla put her hands on her hips. "And you weren't invited to the rehearsal dinner, so why are you here?"

"He wants you back." The tension rolling off Jonah was palpable; she could feel his gaze on the side of her face, burning. "Realized he's a fucking dumbass, and he wants you back."

"He's right." Geoff put his hands in the pockets of his pleated khaki pants. She'd thought she'd gotten rid of all of them, but they kept coming back like the villain in a horror movie. *Why on earth did her ex look so relaxed?* Could he not feel the coiled alpha-male energy at her side, just about ready to snap? "I was sitting at home tonight, and I realized how much I missed you."

"You wanted to sit home every night." She couldn't believe she'd actually bought his line about her being boring. In that moment, looking at how small Geoff was, she realized that he had been projecting his own sense of inadequacy when he dumped her. "You need to leave before the rest of the family gets out of the restaurant."

"They were almost my family, too."

"But they're not." Jonah's words were sharp, and Geoff started. "Hector fired you, didn't he?"

The wince on Geoff's face told her that was probably true. "Carla, who is this guy? You're just bringing a friend, right? Like one of those inappropriate guys you dated before me." Geoff took a step closer to her, and she backed up. Jonah put his arm around her waist, catching her close. "You couldn't possibly be serious about this guy?"

"I—" Carla struggled to find the words to describe how she felt about Jonah. Even though she was annoyed with him at the moment, Jonah felt essential to her in a way that Geoff never had. Despite the fact that they bickered and liked to needle each other, she felt a comfort with Jonah that she didn't even know with her family sometimes. And her lust for Jonah was undeniable every time they touched. Her pregnancy might be an accident, but being with Jonah wasn't.

Her heart raced and her lips parted as the genuine, unvarnished truth rushed through her.

She loved him, but she couldn't say that to her ex before she said it to Jonah. She didn't want to say that she cared about him, because that was too small to describe what he did to her. Maybe she could say that she needed him, but they needed each other.

"You had your chance. Your chance is over." Those two simple sentences, in Jonah's quiet growl stopped everything. Carla had never been a woman who wanted to be claimed; that's why she'd dated guys who didn't want strings before she was with Geoff. Hell, she chose Geoff because she knew he wouldn't make her feel anything. And then she let him make her feel small. Regardless, she loved the feeling of Jonah surrounding her, not making her fade into the background, but holding her up.

"Is that true, Carla?" Geoff looked defeated, but he must have held out hope that he could manipulate her into taking him back. She nodded. "He's not good enough for you."

Before she had a chance to deny it, Jonah said, "Well, you're definitely not good enough for Carla. I'm going to take my chances."

Tears welled up in Carla's eyes. Stupid hormones making her cry when she was happy. Elation coursed through her at the feeling of Jonah having her back.

"So, that's it?"

"That's it." Carla nearly apologized, but left the "I'm sorry" off this time. She'd apologized to Geoff all the time, simply for being who she was. And she was done being sorry for that.

Geoff stood there for a minute, as though he was waiting for her to tack on an apology. When she stood her ground and said nothing, he turned and walked away. With every step he took away from her, she felt stronger.

Jonah crowded around her closer, the adrenaline of the confrontation likely leaving his body. She let the tears fall then, but didn't say anything. She wasn't sure how she could explain herself.

"Are you okay?" No, she was not okay. "You didn't eat anything. You should eat something for the baby."

Without warning, he dropped to his knees in the parking lot and rested his head against her belly. Probably only because he'd had most of a bottle of scotch with her dad, but she was touched that he was so worried about her. This was a very inconvenient time and place for him to be making big declarations.

She needed to keep the secret about her pregnancy from her parents until after the wedding. Until after he was gone. "Shhhhh. Someone will hear you."

"Are you ashamed that you're having a baby with me?" His eyes looked so sad, and she'd say just about anything to get him to stand up.

"No. No, I'm so glad." It was true. Not right now, but true. "How much scotch did you drink?"

"Maybe, like two." *Lies. All lies.*

"Two drinks? No wonder you turned down all the mojitos I tried to mix in Cuba."

He shook his head, his face buried again in her dress. Voices were coming closer. Her family had closed down the restaurant, so it had to be them. "Two bottles." His words were muffled enough.

"Are you insane?"

"No." He looked up at her, putting one foot on the ground and then the other so she was looking up at him again. He cupped her face in his hands and kissed her forehead. She thanked God for small favors that he didn't try her mouth. She didn't want to explain why she'd puked all over her date when she hadn't even had champagne during the toasts. "You gotta eat more. I can't be around all the time to make sure you eat."

"If you walk to the car, I promise I'll eat some toast when I get home."

She'd been so nervous about what her father would think of Jonah that she'd barely touched her dinner. When her mother had noticed that and the fact that she wasn't drinking, she'd had to think fast. She'd told her that she was doing a last-minute cleanse because her bridesmaid's dress didn't quite fit. Her mother had been skeptical because it was clear that Carla was actually thinner than normal—what with all the nausea and the absence of alcohol in her diet. She'd tell her mother after the wedding, when everything calmed down.

Jonah put his arm over her shoulders, and they were a few feet from the car when Cole and Javi caught up with them. They each grabbed one arm.

"Thanks, guys." Carla ran over to the driver's side and let them figure out how to get him in the car. They sat Jonah down in the passenger seat, with the door open.

"Thanks, guys. Can you do me another favor?" Jonah paused, as though he was going to ask one of them for a kidney, "Make her eat when I have to go away to work. My baby's going to be huge, and she needs to eat more."

Carla stilled. She never would have expected him to say that.

Javi and Cole peered at her through the car window, shock etched on both their faces.

"Baby?" It wasn't often her brother had this little to say, but now was one of those times. They'd had a lot of scotch; it was a bad idea to have this conversation here and now. Considering the damage Javi had done to Cole's face when he found out the former Navy SEAL was *dating* Alana, she didn't want this to escalate.

"Shhh." Carla looked around the vicinity of the car, for her parents. Hopefully, they were still inside, settling the tab.

"Baby?" It was as though her brother's brain had shorted out. By the time he said it again, Alana and Maya were at the car.

"Oh no," Alana said, her eyes big. "I thought we were keeping this a secret until after the wedding."

Carla got out of the car, and Javi grabbed Jonah, jerking him out of the passenger seat.

"Baby?" Javi's fist, the one that wasn't holding Jonah's jacket, clenched. Maya grabbed Javi's arm and stopped him from punching Jonah. "Papi, you have to calm down before your parents get out here."

Javi grunted and then let Jonah go so abruptly he stumbled before catching himself. Jonah held up his hands, seeming sober for the first time in a few hours. "I know you didn't want me to tell them."

"No. I didn't." Carla sighed and wrapped her arms around her waist, feeling exposed.

"Why didn't you want me to tell them?"

She did not want to have this conversation here. As much as she now realized that she wanted her relationship with Jonah to be about more than sharing parenting duties, this public airing of grievances wasn't working for her. "This is Alana's weekend. I don't want it to be about me."

Her family hadn't backed off, and they were running out of time before her parents would come out of the restaurant wondering what was wrong. Javi's fists were still clenching, and he still had a glaze of anger over his face. He was so jacked up that he'd probably spill the beans unless Maya got him in a taxi immediately.

Carla felt nauseous, so much so that she bent over and put her head on the cool metal of the car's trunk. Immediately, her sister rushed over. "Are you okay? Is everything okay with the baby?"

Jonah came over, too. "Oh, God. Oh no. Please tell me I didn't fuck things up again."

"Calm down, everyone. I'm just going to wait until I don't feel like puking anymore."

Jonah rubbed a hand up and down her back, which instantly made her feel better. All of the sounds of her siblings and their partners talking in hushed tones faded away. She tried to block out everything but Jonah's touch, the concern in his voice. "I don't know what I'd do if anything happened to the baby."

"What baby?" Her father's roar of anger echoed off the concrete walls that surrounded the lot. Her father had clearly taken part in the lion's share of that scotch because he only got that loud when he was really angry or had had too much to drink. Lucky her, tonight it was a bit of both. Neither happened often, especially when it came to her. Being the baby of the family had one advantage, and that was the fact that she had to work really hard to make her father angry. "What did I tell you about getting my daughter pregnant?"

Jonah's hand jerked off her back, and it got her to stand up. Her father had him in a headlock, something that wouldn't have been possible if Jonah had laid off the booze, just a tad.

"Daddy, stop!" Her father didn't listen. He started spitting out Spanish swear words faster than she could translate them in her head. She might be fluent, but she wasn't a native speaker. But even though she couldn't keep up, she knew it was getting nasty.

Jonah didn't even look like he was fighting. She wanted to go over to them, make them stop, but her sister held her shoulders. "Our family is so classy," Alana said.

Her mother rushed over to her with one word. "Baby?"

Carla dropped her head forward and nodded. "Baby."

Her mom squealed and threw her arms around her; she almost lost her breath from the tightness of the hug. She had not been expecting this kind of reaction from either of her parents. But she couldn't be happy about the fact that her mom seemed excited about her being knocked up—either that or she'd had a lot of wine—because her father and the father of her baby were now rolling around on a greasy car park.

"Stop it." Still, they didn't react. Jonah grunted when her father got a shot in to his kidneys and rolled on top of Jonah. When her father pulled back his fist, Carla pushed her mother away. "Stop them."

Her mother didn't seem inclined to do much because she said, "Don't break his face too much."

Carla pointed at her brother. "Javi, do something." She looked at Cole who seemed to be trying real hard not to double over with laughter. "Cole?"

Both of them held up their hands. "You think your father wouldn't have beat the shit out of me had I gotten Alana knocked up—well, knocked up before our honeymoon next week? I guess a beatdown is the price of admission in this family."

Even tough-as-shit Maya winced when they heard bones crunch as her father made contact with Jonah's face. She looked at Javi. "I'm really glad I couldn't get you pregnant if I tried."

Jesus. Carla had never seen her father this mad before. He hadn't even blinked when Geoff had dumped her. He'd just quietly *fired* him for publicly humiliating her apparently. But she guessed this wasn't the same thing. Geoff hadn't embarrassed the family by dumping her. He'd only embarrassed her.

Anger filled her chest, and she shook off Alana's hold to march over to the two tussling, grunting figures. She wished Jonah would pin her father to the ground and end this right now. They were having a baby, and she needed him to stand up for her—for their family.

She kicked one of them. Right now, she didn't care much who. "Stop it."

"Get back." Jonah's words were wheezy because her father punched him in the side. "You'll hurt the baby."

"Stop fighting or I'll separate you myself." Hearing her so close to the edge and the possibility of hurting her must have finally gotten through because they stopped fighting. Both of them flopped on the ground on their backs.

"Daddy, you're going to give yourself a heart attack." She pointed at her own chest. "This is my fault. Jonah only came to the wedding to help me out. I just wanted you to know who he was and maybe not hate him."

Her father sat up and made like he was going to hit Jonah again. Jonah didn't even move, not even a flinch. He clearly thought that this was his fault. "You aren't even going to marry her?"

"That's not how this works. That's not how any of this works." Maya looked at Javi. "*Su familia esta loca.*" Carla would have laughed at Maya's commentary in the background—especially the part where she added, "If your dick was even a little bit smaller, I swear to God I would leave all your asses in my rearview"—if this whole situation wasn't quite so ridiculous and so public. Carla wished, more than anything, that she wasn't related to these people right now.

Her family might not be famous, but a few local gossip blogs would be eager to post this security cam video. All she needed on top of being dumped publicly was to have her baby daddy and her father go viral for the dumbest, drunkest street fight ever. She might have wrapped her head around unwed motherhood, but this was too trashy by a mile.

"He's not going to marry you?" Carla turned to her mother. She sounded confused, like of course they were going to get married because she was pregnant. She'd never seen her mother's forehead crease that much.

"No, he's just my date to the wedding." Carla wanted to get in her car and drive away. Jonah could stay here and fight with her family about her.

She had to be in love with that man; it was the only thing that could explain how much hatred for him she had burning inside her at the moment— the hatred that made humiliation singe her inside. "Of course we're not getting married, we don't even really like each other. I'd rather die."

Her belly knotted with regret the instant she said it. Her mother gasped, and her sister and her sister-in-law mumbled to their men. But no one said anything.

Carla didn't dare turn around and look at Jonah. She knew what this had to sound like to him, that she—like Katie—would literally rather die than marry him. This wasn't the first time a thoughtless moment or phrase had gotten her into trouble, but this was certainly the worst. *She* was certainly the worst.

"Hector, get up." Her mother's words were sharp. She took the tone that always meant Javi was grounded for a month.

Her father followed instructions and came up alongside her. Carla could feel the disappointment rolling off him in waves. She'd always thought she'd let her parents down by not being smart enough with numbers, by not being as perfect or as brilliant as her older siblings. She'd thought she'd owned that part of herself, and forgiven her parents for not seeing her as valuable. But she'd never given them reason to be disappointed like this before. Right now, she could *feel* their disappointment, and she had never felt so worthless or so alone in her entire life.

She couldn't look at either of them as they walked away without saying another word. She stayed where she was, still.

Finally, she mustered a glance at Jonah. He didn't move either. His silence spoke volumes. He'd believed her when she'd said she trusted him. And now he thought she'd lied to him. He wouldn't forgive her for this. He shouldn't.

Jonah deserved a woman who would stand up for him. He deserved better than this. Than her. He'd shown her so much care and compassion when she'd needed it. She couldn't even repay him by lying to her family for just a while, for making him feel like he could be part of that.

He was certainly part of her right now. Carla put her hand over her lower belly. Only then did he heave himself off the ground. His steps toward her were slow. When he came up behind her, he wouldn't touch her. She stepped back, needing his touch, but he moved away. He wouldn't touch her ever again, and it felt like something inside her split open and spilled all over the ground.

"Turn around." His voice was soft. "Please turn around."

She did, and he rubbed his fist against his chest. "Listen, I didn't—" He put a hand up, and she stopped speaking. Her vision of him blurred as tears gathered.

"You don't even *like* me?" His voice was soft and flat. Someone his size should never sound like a lost little boy. She'd done this. She'd reduced him to this.

"I do. I just—I wanted him to stop."

"He would have stopped. He didn't even hit me that hard." When she looked over the quickly forming bruises on his face, his ripped shirt, she tended to disagree. "Well, I'm not going to piss blood in the morning."

He might have meant it as a joke, but his mouth didn't curve into a smile. "I didn't mean to say that last thing. That's not true." But she'd said it, and she could see the damage. No apology would be enough, but she had to try. "I'm sorry." Two hollow words when he'd trusted her with his heart and soul, and she'd pretended it didn't mean anything. All to save face in front of her family. Unlike her family, he'd always made her feel special, cherished. She really was as weak as she had been when they'd first met. She was willing to wound someone who had been good to her almost from the start, just so she wouldn't be embarrassed. "You didn't want to marry me."

Color crawled up his neck, telling her that maybe he had wanted more with her. Her breath caught as hope jolted through her. Maybe he had wanted to stay a permanent part of her and the baby's life.

"I didn't know." He dropped his head. "Now, I guess I do. You don't even like me."

He leaned against her car and pulled his cell phone out of his pocket. "I'm going to get a car."

"No, let me drive you home."

"I'm going to a hotel."

"Please don't. Come home with me. We'll figure this out."

He turned his back to her. "You're sure everything's all right with the baby?"

Tears spilled out again, faster than she could wipe them from her face. His concern touched her even though he was about to hit the road. When he finally met her look, his eyes were cold. She could have been looking at a stranger. The night that Geoff had tossed her off, she hadn't even cried. She'd looked around the restaurant and seen too many people she knew to make a spectacle of herself. Now, she wanted to drop to her knees and beg Jonah not to leave her. If she did that, and he stayed, it wouldn't be because he wanted to. If he stayed and tried to work this out, she would only find a way to fuck things up again.

"Come home with me. Please."

"I don't want to go with you. I want you to go home to your perfect condo and your perfect life."

"It's not perfect. You're not there." Her tears started to fall, and she no longer cared about humiliating herself. He walked toward her but didn't take her arm. She knew that he wanted her to get in the car and drive away. She thought about standing in his way, pulling his face down to hers, and kissing him, telling him with her body that she liked him, that she wanted him. She loved him.

She took a step toward him, and he backed away as though her touch would burn him.

"Get in the damned car, and go." His words were so flat and cold that they felt like a door slamming on all the possibility she'd felt with him the night before.

He didn't want her, and she didn't deserve him.

So she did the only thing she could do and turned around and got into the car. Once he had seen she was belted, he shut the door. Leaving her in deadly silence.

Chapter 21

Jonah hated hotels almost as much as he hated hangovers that set in before he went to sleep. Unfortunately, he was dealing with both. And the pain behind his eyes and the antiseptic smell of the sheets in this prison cell of his own making paled in comparison to the hole in his chest Carla had left.

He wasn't a foolish romantic boy anymore. He'd thought he'd been long past getting pulled in by a sweet girl with lots of issues. But apparently he hadn't learned what he'd needed to from his history, and he had been doomed to repeat it.

As soon as he'd gotten checked in, he'd texted one of his reporter buddies. Brian had asked Jonah to go back to Syria with him, and he'd had to turn him down to go to the wedding. Before tonight—especially given the news about the baby—Jonah hadn't wanted to go back. Ever since he'd found out he was going to be a father, he'd been thinking of leaving the news business behind and calling Charlie about that travel show. Now, he didn't have any reason not to go back to what he'd been doing for years. He no longer had a woman—or a family—to consider.

He needed to get his life back on track—the lonely track he'd set for himself after leaving school.

He didn't have any of his stuff; that was all at Carla's, but he needed to wash the cigar smoke off. He'd grabbed a tube of toothpaste and some mouthwash from the gift shop downstairs so he could get the taste of whisky and tobacco out of his mouth. He showered, wanting to wash the whole night off of his skin. But it didn't work. He didn't feel like himself anymore. Being with Carla had changed him.

He picked up his phone and checked for calls. Brian had texted him back with flight information, but he wished Carla had called. He didn't know what they could talk about. Hearing her say that she'd rather die than be with him had knocked him for a loop. He'd pegged Carla as a spoiled rich girl, but he hadn't pegged her as thoughtless and cruel until tonight. She could say that she didn't mean it, but she'd cut him open standing in that parking garage. He'd looked around, surprised not to see his guts splattered all over the pavement.

He crawled into bed because he should get some sleep before he left in the morning, but he couldn't stop thinking about how stupid he was to fall for a woman who didn't want him, who saw him as a means to an end. What had happened with Katie, and the aftermath, had been devastating. The aching in his chest and the feeling of emptiness inside told him that forgetting Carla would be just as hard. Still, after she'd tossed him aside in front of her whole family, he wanted to feel her skin against his.

So, he lay in a hotel bed, wishing he was with her while hating her guts.

He wasn't going to peace out like his father had, but would Carla even let him see the kid? Or would her father's lawyers find a way to shut him out? Maybe they'd both be better off if he disappeared.

Somehow, he must have dozed off with all of those questions in his head because he woke up to pounding on his door. The room was still dark, so he probably hadn't been asleep for too long.

He put his pants back on and hobbled over to the door. He'd lied to Carla; Hector had put a hurting on him, and he would be stiff for days. When he looked through the peephole, he was shocked to see Lola standing there in a white suit, spine straight, ready to kick ass.

"Open the door, *mijo*."

His scotch-soured stomach churned as he followed instructions, but when she pushed her way into the room he said, "I'm not your son. What are you doing here?"

Lola grabbed the torn shirt he'd been wearing the night before from the end of the bed and sniffed it. Her face scrunched up in disgust.

"Saving you from yourself." She threw his shirt at him. She had a good arm for someone in her sixties. "And going to my niece's wedding."

"I don't need saving." Carla had saved him from both of themselves.

"Yes, you do." She rolled her eyes. "Otherwise, you wouldn't have been rolling around a parking lot with Hector at his daughter's rehearsal dinner."

"How do you even know about that?" He buttoned up his wrinkled shirt. "When did you even get here?"

She looked at him as though he was stupid, probably a good thing because he felt plenty stupid right now. "Do you have better clothes than that?"

He shook his head. "At Carla's."

Lola's eyes went wide. "Well, you can't go there right now. You broke her heart."

"I think you have things reversed."

"How so?" Lola propped one hand on her hip, a knowing smile on her face. "How did she break your heart?"

"She said she'd rather die than marry me." *God, he sounded so girly.* "Did she mean it?"

"No, but I told her about Katie, and she still *said* it."

Lola walked over and sat in the desk chair, crossing her legs elegantly, letting him know she wasn't leaving until the situation resolved itself to her satisfaction. "Did she apologize?"

"Yes, but she shouldn't have said it."

Lola inclined her head to the side. "Sort of like you said things you shouldn't have to Katie? Things you couldn't take back. Things you meant at the time."

"She doesn't even like me."

"Ha!" Lola clapped her hands together and threw her head back. "That girl has more than liked you since you met. She says one stupid thing, and it's all over? You're going to lose your woman and your baby because she said one stupid thing?"

Jonah sat on the edge of the bed. "She's better off."

"Both of you children are very dumb." Lola patted his head. "As soon as I get to Hector's house, after dinner with my kids, he's raging and screaming at the walls."

"Because I fucked up." His shoulders slumped forward.

"No, because both of you 'fucked up.'"

"I don't blame the guy for losing his shit. I got his daughter pregnant. It wasn't supposed to be a thing. It was just going to be a one-night stand."

"That's the dumbest thing I've ever heard. The first night I saw you together, I knew that you were for each other." Lola let out a rueful bark of a laugh. "I know you don't like to feel obligated to anyone. But I know you, and you don't give up when something's right."

Lola was wrong. He'd given up on relationships a long time ago. And he'd absolutely given up on relationships with coddled, fickle women like Carla. "She doesn't even like me."

"She does, too."

"Then why was she using me as a scapegoat for her pregnancy?"

"That's not what she was doing." Lola flicked him in the back of his head. "Carla—she's a special person. She's not like her brother and sister. She's not like her father, or even her mother. She only wants to make things around her beautiful."

"I don't see what this has to do with me." Usually he had patience for Lola's detours and digressions, but not right now. He got to his feet, but she grabbed his hand so he couldn't walk away.

"It has *everything* to do with you." She sat next to him and patted his hand. "The thing between you and Carlita is beautiful. I saw it the first night she got to the island. She never belonged with that stupid boy who dumped her. She belongs with someone like you who wasn't about to let her off the hook for every damned thing—someone who wasn't going to let her spark die."

He sat back down, and she let go of his hand.

"I thought—when it was just us alone—I thought we could try to make something work. But family is everything to her, and they hate me."

"Hector hates you, but Hector hates everyone." She grabbed his hand again.

Jonah could see that, and hope cleared some of the fog in his brain. But he didn't see the point if Carla didn't want him as much as he wanted her.

"She doesn't need me."

Lola pinched him and gave him one of her rare sour looks. "Of course she needs you. She needs someone like you to challenge her. She needs someone like you to treat her gently. My family, we are not soft people. Even Carla's mother is tough. Carla's never felt like she measured up." Lola put her pointer finger in his face. "But you see her for who she is. As soon as I saw you together," she clapped her hands together sharply, "I knew that you would be good for Carlita."

His heart beat faster. "I'm leaving in a few hours."

"No, you're not."

"I have a job."

Lola stood up, smiling at him. "You have a more important job." She patted his cheeks. With him sitting, she was just about at eye level. "You're going to be a father."

His stomach lurched again. She winked at him as she walked toward the door, opening the door before stopping. "You're going to figure things out. You'll forgive her, and she'll forgive you."

"She was crying, and I made her go."

"You'll make it up to her."

And then she walked out and closed the door behind her.

Jonah stood up, blood coursing through his veins and his legs anxious to move. He wasn't sure what to do with everything she'd said. Jonah knew how to leave. That's what had always worked for him.

If he wanted to be enough for Carla, if he was the man Lola thought he was, he would have to stick it out. He and Carla would have to learn to get angry with each other and talk about it instead of blowing up their lives. She would have to learn to be careful with him, and he would have to do the same with her. Their baby deserved two parents who loved her—and who could learn to love each other without it hurting all the time. He wanted that much more than he wanted to leave.

Now, he had to teach himself how to stay.

* * * *

How was it possible that she dragged herself out of bed?

Carla felt as though she'd been hit by a semitruck when she showed up at the hotel suite their mother had reserved for getting ready at around nine. They were all going to get made up and dressed, and Carla needed as much time for makeup as humanly possible. As she'd parked her car, she wondered if it was possible to get a face transplant for the day.

Between the not sleeping and the constant pukey feeling she had going on, the bags under her eyes, and the green tint to her skin, she felt epically ugly.

"You look terrible," Maya said when Carla opened the door to the suite. She didn't even have the energy to come up with a snappy comeback for her beautiful, honest future sister-in-law. And she looked particularly gorgeous today—without a stitch of makeup on. Carla hated her.

"Thanks."

Maya took Carla's dress bag to hang in the closet. "I'm going to get you some tea and me a mimosa, then, you're going to tell me everything."

Carla looked around for her sister. "Where's Alana?" She felt comfortable telling Maya things that Alana would judge her for. Her future sister-in-law was a judgment-free zone when it came to this kind of thing. Maya had judgments, just not about sex or accidental pregnancies.

"She's still sleeping." Maya pointed to the closed door. "I'm fairly certain that Cole snuck in for a quickie before I got here."

Carla sighed. "Of course he did."

Maya got their drinks, and they both sat on the sofa, facing each other. "I like him."

"Who?"

Maya gave her an "oh please" look. Carla's cheeks burned with shame at how she'd treated Jonah.

"I like him, too."

"Then why did you say you didn't last night?"

"I didn't like him at first." Carla knew those words weren't quite right. "I mean when I showed up at Lola's house, he was all growly and mean. He called me princess. And I wanted to punch him in the face every time he opened his mouth."

"He didn't just roll over and do what you wanted then?" Maya finished her mimosa in short course.

"Slow down there. Alana will kill you if you trip down the aisle."

"Hours until the wedding, and you need my most uncensored advice."

Carla wasn't sure she could handle an uncensored Maya. Censored Maya already told her a lot of things she didn't want to hear.

"I like him now, but I don't think he'll forgive me."

"Both of you need to grow the fuck up. Do you know how many times I want to punch Javi in the face in a week?"

"A hundred." Carla smiled.

"More like a thousand. Your brother is an asshole. He's arrogant, and he's a snob. But he's my arrogant, snobby asshole. And he believes in me and makes me want to be a better person."

"That's really sweet." Carla drank more of her tea, which was actually starting to make her feel better. Javi was so lucky to have Maya. "Jonah's not an asshole. He's actually really sweet."

"Are you trying to tell me the sex is bad with this one, too?" Carla tingled at the memory of sex with Jonah.

Alana had brought her to Javi and Maya's condo the night Geoff had dumped her. Carla had gotten very drunk and explained in great detail how bad her sex life with Geoff had been. And that's when there had actually been a sex life to complain about.

"No, the sex is—incredible. Surprising."

"Like he-tried-to-put-it-in-your-butt-without-asking surprising or good surprising?"

Carla laughed so hard she snorted tea, which felt so good compared to the gnawing sadness she'd felt since the night before.

"Good surprising. And he always asks."

"So, the stuff about him on the Internet isn't true?"

"No, he told me everything. I believe him."

"Well, you probably should have prepped your dad for meeting him better."

Regret made Carla's legs feel restless, so she stood and walked to the window. "You're right. I'm not used to having to stand up to Daddy. I just knew he'd be so disappointed in me when he found out about the baby, and I wanted him to at least meet Jonah before I told him."

"All of you care so much about what your parents think." Maya stood, and poured herself another mimosa, and rigged up the coffee machine to make Carla more tea. "You're all adults, and you get to decide how to live your lives. Your parents, and stupid, local gossip blogs be damned."

"I don't care what they think—I'm already a disappointment."

Maya guffawed. "Your father was only that pissed last night because you *are* his perfect, little princess. You are always helping your mom with stupid luncheons, and you almost married a guy you weren't even into because he worked for your dad."

"But I'm not as smart as Alana or Javi."

"You didn't go to a fancy school, but you're not stupid. And your brother is an idiot. Huge dick, tiny brain."

Carla scrunched up her nose. She knew Maya was just calling her brother stupid to make her feel better; her brother was a genius when he applied himself. "If you keep talking about his dick, I might vomit. No joke. I don't need to know that."

"But I got you to stop thinking about Jonah, didn't I?"

The door of the bedroom opened, and Alana came out into the living space with definite sex hair. Carla tried to put on her best supportive-sister face.

"I need coffee before we talk about what happened last night." Alana wasn't going to let this go either, and it made Carla feel a little more normal. Even though last night had been fucked up, it felt good to have so much support.

Maya made coffee, and Alana pulled Carla over to the couch. "Tell me."

"This is supposed to be your day." She didn't want to need her sister's comfort, but she did. So, she laid her head on her sister's lap.

Alana ran her fingers through Carla's hair like she had when they were kids. "I'm going to be married at the end of it, so it's still my day. *Tell me.*"

"I like him."

"She more than *likes* him," Maya said in a singsong voice before she handed Alana a steaming cup.

Carla wanted to be able to deny it, but she couldn't. It was crazy and impulsive to fall in love with a guy after spending two nights with him and getting accidentally pregnant with his baby. But she was the impulsive one in the family. Maybe, this one time, her impulses were right. "I totally more than like him." Alana's hand stilled.

"What are you going to do about it?" Alana was practical, always wanting a plan.

"Well, I was going to talk to him after the wedding."

"That won't work." Maya sat on the ottoman and shook her head. "He looks like a runner."

Alana pursed her lips, her customary thinking face. "I'm sure Daddy has looked into a hitman to take him out. Maybe we could convince him to switch it over to kidnapping?" Her sister was clearly joking, but Carla had thought of that.

The door opened. A chill went down Carla's spine because it was probably her mother. The way her mom had looked at her the night before had chastened her. She hadn't even tried to call her and explain because she knew that would only cause her mother's temper to explode.

Her mom stopped short, but there was no indication that she was upset on her placid face. "Oh good, you're all here."

Carla stood up and approached her mother, who was near the door. "Listen, I know you're mad at me, but I'm going to fix it."

"Yes, you are." Her mother's facial expression softened, and she hugged Carla tight. "You care about that man, and you hurt him. You have to fix it."

"You're not mad at me for getting pregnant?"

Carla's mom released her from the hug and grabbed her hand. "Let's get me a drink." Carla's mom led her towards the bar, and Maya tipped her glass in a "cheers" motion.

"I was mad that you didn't tell me, when both of these girls knew." She took a long drink. "But I'm getting a grandchild. And you'll be a great mother."

Carla's chest squeezed at her mother's show of faith, but she highly doubted that she'd be a great mother. She might be able to get herself to kind-of-okay, but great would be a stretch.

"Don't make that face. We already have enough to do with it to cover up those dark circles."

"We were just talking about how to fix things with Jonah," Maya said.

Carla rolled her eyes at Maya; she'd been hoping to avoid pulling her mother into this any further. Jonah probably hated her family enough. If he knew that they were all gunning for he and Carla to get back together, he would run hard and far and fast.

"You didn't try to fix things last night?" Her mother sounded shocked.

"He put me in my car and went to a hotel."

"Which one? You need to go talk to him."

"He doesn't want to talk to me right now." The way he'd looked at her last night, she knew he wouldn't want to see her—maybe not ever.

Her mother sat her in an armchair and started putting foundation on her. It reminded Carla of when her mom had put her makeup on for dance competitions; the familiarity of it was intimate and sweet. "I wouldn't want to see you after what you said about him last night either, but you have to make him see you."

"You didn't get this worked up when Geoff dumped me. You didn't demand that I try to get him back or anything."

"That's because he was wrong for you." Her mother put the finishing touches on her foundation and then attacked her with cakey concealer. "You have no idea how relieved your father and I were to lose our deposits on that one."

"Geoff was a douche," Maya said.

"If *People* had a 'Least Sexy Man Alive' award, Geoff would get it." Everyone laughed at Alana's addition.

"Why didn't anyone tell me this?" Carla wanted to jump up, but she wanted to keep her eyeball makeup brush-free even more. "This would have been useful information."

"You are the most stubborn of all my children." Her mother cupped her face. "You seemed determined to marry him."

"I'm more stubborn than Javi? Really?"

Maya piped in, "You're all stubborn."

"I was so upset when Geoff broke things off." Her eyes filled with tears, and her mother shook her head. "Just use waterproof. This is not going to be a tear-free day."

"You were only upset because you were embarrassed." She flushed because her sister knew her too well.

"I was a mess. I didn't leave my house."

"Because you cared too much about what other people thought." Maya was kind of a bitch sometimes, but she was right-on. "It wasn't about the fact that you actually loved the guy."

"Well, the whole unwed-mother thing cured me of embarrassment. I'm going to get kicked out of everything." Carla looked up at the ceiling. She didn't feel anxious at all, just sad and not wanting to be alone.

"Lola got into town last night," her mother said.

"What does that have to do with anything?" Maybe her mother was already drunk.

"Didn't she kind of set the two of you up?"

"Sort of. She left us alone together."

"Then maybe she'll help patch things up." Her mother looked at the makeup palette. "You need a lot more shadow on the eyelids."

Chapter 22

The cavernous church and the smell of flowers and incense sparked a sense of déjà vu in Jonah. He hadn't been to a wedding since he was a kid. He'd declined invitations from friends back home and the guys from college. But he liked how the voices echoed off the walls of the sanctuary to make a kind of music.

He sat in the back pew again, his hands sweating and his feet itching. Lola looked at him from the front of the church every so often, as if she was making sure he was still there. He was surprised she hadn't brought a cattle prod to make sure he stayed. He wouldn't be shocked if Lola encouraged a shotgun wedding if she thought he was being stupid.

His head jerked back when Hector sat next to him and didn't shove a pistol in his still-aching ribcage. "I would have thought you'd leave town by now."

"No, sir." Jonah looked toward the exits, making sure he had a clean getaway if this got ugly like last night. He was less afraid of some warlords than he was of Hector right now.

"I thought that was your MO." Hector had a lot of balls for someone fifty pounds smaller than him.

Jonah scooted away from the other man. "You don't know the whole story."

"I don't, and I'm sorry for hitting you."

"You embarrassed Carla." Jonah was having trouble keeping his voice low. "She hates being embarrassed."

Hector inclined his head. "Well, you do know something about my daughter."

"I know a lot of things about her." Jonah turned on the pew so he was facing Hector, who raised one eyebrow. "I know she is terrified of letting you and her mother down. I know she's compassionate and kind. She's the most organized person I've ever met. I know I care about her more than

I should after the amount of time I've spent with her." Jonah wanted to tell Hector that he loved Carla, that he would do anything for her and his baby. But he wanted to tell Carla that first.

"Are you prepared to stay here in Miami to be with her?"

Jonah tightened his jaw. "That's up to Carla."

"Why aren't you telling her that?"

Because he was sitting next to her father—her father with a mean right hook. "The wedding's about to start."

"Eh, the priest was late yesterday. The maid of honor can be late today. Go find her and make things up."

"She said she doesn't even like me."

"My own wife doesn't like me half the time." Hector laughed at himself. "She loves me, and she wants to kill me."

"So your whole family is crazy?"

"That's why I wanted to kick the shit out of you, why I threatened you."

"Because you are crazy?"

Hector made like he was going to punch him in the arm, and Jonah flinched. "No, because I saw the way she looked at you. I've tried to control my children's choices too much. And she's my baby—I don't have favorites—but she's the one I've worried about the most. I just snapped."

"I'm sure half a bottle of scotch didn't help."

"Go find her..."

Jonah was up before Hector finished his sentence. By the time he got to the vestibule of the church, where all the bridesmaids and Mrs. Hernandez were waiting, he still hadn't figured out what he was going to say.

Carla stood between her sister and Maya, gorgeous in a pastel dress. She looked beautiful and fresh. She was perfect, and she was looking at him like she wanted him to be there. Just then, he realized that he'd been afraid she would change her mind all along. He was in love with her. It was crazy—maybe he was crazy—maybe just crazy enough to be part of her family.

"Princess, we have to talk."

* * * *

"I've got to get my sister married." Carla's heart beat so fast she was sure she was having a heart attack when she saw Jonah standing in the doorway to the sanctuary. She never thought she'd get to see him looking at her like was right now again. And she was full—her heart, her head. So many things she wanted to say to him were poised to spill out, but this wasn't the right time for that.

Alana pushed her arm. "Go talk to him in the bride's room."

"But this is your day." Carla kept looking at Jonah while she said it. He looked delicious in a suit. Even better than if he was in jeans and a T-shirt. "I thought you were going to leave."

"We've got to talk about that, princess."

"Go." This time her sister used the not-to-be-argued-with voice.

Carla walked over to Jonah, and grabbed his hand. When he smiled at her, something inside snapped loose. She yanked his hand, and he followed.

She took him to the bride's room, and he closed the door behind them. He leaned on it as though he was afraid she'd try to run.

"I do like you." She wanted to get that out of the way first.

"You do? Why'd you say you didn't last night?"

"This was all moving so fast. You were there with my family, and then Geoff was there. I was overwhelmed." She looked down at the white bouquet in her hands. "I wanted my dad to stop hitting you. I was tired, nauseous, overwhelmed."

"Who cares if it's fast if it's right?" He moved to her, kneeling down.

"You're not going to propose, are you?" She didn't want him to do that because she'd know it was out of obligation.

"No." He shook his head and pulled the flowers out of her hands, set them aside on a table. Her heartbeat quickened, and she brushed his hair back with her fingers. "Not now."

"Why didn't you leave?"

"I was about to get on a plane when Lola showed up."

"Oh, God. She didn't threaten you, too?"

"No, but she talked some sense into me." He laced his fingers through hers. "She made me realize that I'd been hiding from feeling anything for anyone for a long time."

"Since Katie." Her stomach dropped. Maybe he was here to say good-bye. Maybe he was going to tell her that he wanted to keep on hiding. She wasn't sure she could take that. "I don't want to force you to be with me—with us."

"I want to be with you." He looked up at her, and her limbs tingled. "I want to be with both of you." He touched her stomach.

Carla's knees went melty and she sank down to the floor with him. He kissed her, hard, flooding her body with relief. She pulled back to say, "Just don't touch my hair, okay?"

He laughed, and it was dark and lusty. "How much time do we have before we get busted by a priest?"

"Ten minutes?" She kissed his jaw and his throat, leaving trails of her lipstick. She didn't care. The whole church full of people here—the same ones who had gossiped about her getting dumped—could see her makeup smeared. She needed him right now.

She unbuttoned Jonah's shirt, needing his warm flesh, his smell against her. He lost the jacket before pulling up her dress. He grasped her thighs, and she ached to feel him inside her. When he cupped her breasts, and kissed her right above the line of her dress, she sighed.

"We're in a church."

"I know." She drew back slightly, worried that this crossed a line for him, even though he wasn't super-Catholic anymore. "Does that bother you?"

"No. Not touching you for over twelve hours bothers me. God might strike me dead, but I'll die happy."

He groaned when she unbuttoned his shirt and pulled the tails out of his pants, and she realized that she must have yanked on his cock. She put her hand over him, and he rocked into her palm.

"Even if you didn't like me, I'd still want you."

"I like you. I'm afraid I've caught feelings for you."

He palmed her silk panties, laced his finger though the side to touch her. "Even if you didn't like me, I could get you this wet. I would make you come until you caught feelings for me."

"What else would you do?"

With the other hand, the one that wasn't nudging at her entrance, he pulled down both straps of her dress. "I'd worship you here," he said, before running his tongue around her nipples. She yanked at his belt, but he moved his hips away to stop her. "Just let me make you come. Let me."

"You should know that I'm a terrible listener." She pulled his belt loose and slipped the button from his fly with two fingers. "And I'm really horny because I didn't get my morning sex."

"That's your fault. You said you didn't like me." He ran his teeth over one nipple as she was pulling down his zipper.

"Totally my fault, but are you complaining?" She pulled his pants and underwear down to his knees and gave his bare cock a hard stroke.

"I'm not going to complain when your hand's on my dick." He pulled his hands free of her panties and laid her down on the floor.

"We're in a church. This is filthy. We're going to hell, for sure." He grunted, somehow maneuvering the dress up so it wouldn't get too wrinkled. She found his cock again and stroked until he was cursing.

"We weren't already going to hell for fucking in your great aunt's kitchen?" He had a point.

He slid inside her, and her eyes rolled back in their sockets. Her mouth opened and closed until he found her with another kiss and started to move inside her. When he finally released her so they could both breathe, she whispered, "Yes, yes, yes," on each stroke.

"I was in hell before I met you." How could he talk right now? "Alone, and I thought I liked that."

She grabbed his face and made him look at her. "You're not alone. You'll never be alone."

"You like me?" His mouth curled into that filthy smile again, and he fucked her harder, deeper, until she was almost without words.

But not quite. Everything in her centered on the feelings unfolding in her chest and her center. Jonah was inside of her, and he'd burrowed his way in the moment he'd opened her aunt's front door in Havana, when he carried her down the street, when he'd trusted her with the worst thing that had happened to him. The awesome power of knowing she could hurt this giant man with her words made her want to say how she felt out loud. "I love you."

She was afraid he would stop when she said that, but she couldn't keep the words in. He didn't. If anything, it spurred him on. They were both incoherent. She was sure she'd leave bruises to rival the ones from his fight last night, but she needed him to be marked as surely as she was.

Her orgasm came by surprise, and he put his hand over her mouth so she could yell into it. He went over seconds later, his face contorting into pleasure.

He kissed her just as she started giggling. She stopped when he pulled back with a serious look on his face. "I love you too, princess."

"Good."

* * * *

Carla's mother had gotten the waiting guests enough champagne while they were waiting that, if any of them noticed her looking disheveled, none of them said anything. When she walked up the aisle behind Maya, Jonah was sitting in the front pew, with Lola.

Her great aunt winked and waggled her eyebrows, which almost caused Carla to lose her composure. During the entire mass, she and Jonah snuck looks at each other.

Two months ago, she'd had no future. She was the one nobody wanted— no real job, no love, no idea what to do. She went to Cuba thinking she could at least get the job right.

She hadn't.

Instead, she had something better.

When Jonah pulled her out on the dance floor at the reception, she wasn't looking at everyone else, wondering what they thought of her. She was looking at him.

And when he kissed her, she had everything.

Epilogue

"You guys okay if I take Layla to the beach for an hour?" Charlie was cradling her daughter and bouncing her on his hip as though he was a pro and not a bachelor.

"Make sure to cover her in sunscreen," Jonah said. "It's in the go—diaper—bag I packed."

"Cool. Cool." Charlie scooped up the bag. "Do you guys need more than an hour?"

"Yes, but he gets antsy if he's away from her for longer than that."

Charlie laughed. "What a softie."

"Thanks, Charlie." Carla lowered her voice so that only Jonah could hear. "Takes one to know one."

Charlie had Layla in her stroller and out the door before Carla turned to her man with lustful intent.

"Are you at all disturbed by the fact that he's probably using our daughter to meet women?" Jonah's brow creased with worry.

Carla shook her head again. She wasn't upset—Charlie was now family. And if it gave her an hour alone with her man, she wasn't about to complain.

"Layla will be fine with her Uncle Charlie." Carla tried to tug Jonah down the hall into their bedroom. They had it to themselves for an hour, two, if they were lucky.

Jonah grumbled. "The last time he watched her, he gave her chocolate."

"Babe, you have to lighten up. She's going to get food that we don't keep in the house eventually, and it wasn't that much." Carla turned to face Jonah and slid her hand beneath his T-shirt, rubbing at the skin above his jeans. "We need some alone time."

Layla was six months old, and between a new baby and her new job hosting a travel show with Jonah, Carla didn't have enough of her man these days. Although her mother and sister would take the baby with nothing but a phone call, Jonah didn't like being away from her.

"I thought he was here to talk about the Fiji show." He shook his head. "I don't like the nanny the show sent last time."

It might make her a sick puppy, but it made her so hot when Jonah was an overprotective papa bear. She knew that he was worried that he would be a crap father before the baby was born, but he was a natural.

She pulled him by the belt toward their bedroom. He stopped and put his hands on his hips.

"Why do you do that?" she asked.

"Do what?"

"Get all worried about our daughter when you know it makes me so horny?"

Jonah huffed out a breath, and she felt the resistance drain out of him like a leaky tire. He turned on his gazillion-dollar sexy smile, and she knew she'd won. She pulled harder on his shirt and he leaned down to kiss her.

He didn't kiss her like a concerned father; he kissed her like a caveman, claiming her. She ate it up, pressed her body against his. When she felt his erection, she knew that all of his resistance was for show.

She pulled back and pinched his nipple through his shirt. "You did that on purpose."

"Ow. What?"

"You pretended to be worried about leaving Layla with Charlie for a minute to turn me on."

He didn't deny it. He ran his palms up and down her sides. "You got a problem with that?"

Carla shook her head, and pressed herself against him then. He palmed her ass, lifted her up. "We should get into the bedroom."

"Hold on." He pulled her closer, smelled her hair.

"Resume the kissing, please."

Jonah did one better, throwing her over his shoulder and dragging her into the bedroom. He dropped her on the bed, and then fell to his knees between her legs. He flipped up her short sundress and divested her of her panties with one hand.

"Are you in a hurry?

He pressed her legs open and put a palm on her belly. She wasn't back to what she had been before, but he didn't seem to care about a belly pouch. Meeting Jonah, being with him, having his baby had torn off the mask she'd worn her whole life. It had ripped her apart and reconstituted her into someone else, someone who had more to give than she'd ever given herself credit for.

"You seemed to need to get off, princess." He trailed kisses up her inner thighs, until she arched into the place he held her down. "I'll always get you what you need."

And then he did.

* * * *

Carla was a high-maintenance woman, but Jonah didn't give a fuck. She was his, and she'd given him the best thing. At first, even after they'd decided to give this a shot, he'd been terrified of being a father. But, as soon as he saw Layla's wrinkly little pink face, he was done worrying about how he would do.

All he cared about now were his two girls.

That's why he did a rush job on his and Carla's quickie. He wanted his girls together, both where he could see them. He'd make sure Carla got taken care of later, when the baby went to bed.

When Charlie got back, he had company—most of the Hernandez family. Jonah'd had a hard time getting used to constant visits from his in-laws—or future in-laws—when he'd first moved down to Miami.

He didn't even get to hold Layla and make sure Charlie hadn't done any permanent damage before Alana scooped her up.

Layla was the most agreeable little lady in the world. She was certainly passed around to more relatives in the next hour than any other baby. Even hard-assed Hector took a whole fifteen minutes, and that was after she tugged on his beard.

He found Carla in the kitchen. "What are they doing here, and when are they going to leave?"

"They miss us, and we're leaving again in a few days." She grabbed a beer from the fridge for him and winked. "Make nice."

She sipped a glass of wine. The way the waning light hit her hair filled his heart so much that he would have pulled away from it once. "I love you."

"I know." She winked.

"Marry me."

Then she choked. "We—we already have a baby together."

"That's why you should marry me." He ran his fingers through her hair at the back of her neck. "We'll do it in Fiji. Use the producers and Layla as witnesses. You don't even have to tell anybody we did it."

He knew Carla might be embarrassed that she hadn't ended up with the right guy who had the right job and the perfectly conventional life she'd planned for. It surprised him when she said, "Oh, I'm telling everyone."

"Just not your family right now. Then, they'll never leave."

Don't miss another great Lyrical Press series!

Beautiful Criminal

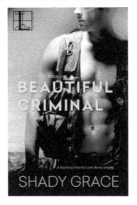

Long days, precious nights . . .

Mima Etu lives a quiet life with her sled dogs in the stunning Canadian Rockies. But that all changes when she stumbles upon a plane crash while out on a supply run. She's shocked to discover the pilot is still alive—though barely. With the sun setting and the temperatures quickly dropping, Mima knows he'd never survive the trip to the nearest hospital. So she takes the stranger back to her cabin. As he heals, his vague answers to Mima's questions about the flight tell her he has secrets. But more disturbing is the consuming, immediate attraction she senses between them.

Before he lost control of his Cessna and plunged into a pilot's hell, Gabriel Miller was on a deadly mission with precious cargo. Now he's awakened in the comfort of a log cabin with a gorgeous woman tending to his every need. Her soft-spoken beauty sparks his longing for a different kind of life…and it isn't long before they surrender to a blazing passion. But their blissful days are numbered. For the owners of the cargo are bent on finding Gabriel—and once they do, they don't intend to leave any witnesses behind.

Visit us at www.kensingtonbooks.com

Prologue

Gabe guided his Cessna 172 Skyhawk as low as he dared over Athabasca River, headed toward Victoria, British Columbia. His boss, Colton McCoy wanted the merchandise delivered by early evening, and time was running short. Due to thick clouds and wind gusts, he'd set off from the private airport near Edmonton two hours later than scheduled, and now, as ice fog overtook the windshield, he wished the flight was canceled all together. Every muscle in his body was as tight as a drawn elastic trying to keep the damn plane level. Most pilots worth their salt knew the Great White North had a mind of its own and the weather could change from pretty to shitty in a second.

Tired of this shit was an understatement. He'd put his life on the line for McCoy too many times. He'd broken necks and busted wallets for the old man. Delivered drugs to every corner of this godforsaken earth. Took a bullet one too many times. And he was dead tired of it all. But this was his job and Gabe owed Colton his life.

An uneasy feeling festered in his gut, a warning this trip would end up worst than the last, but turning back now wasn't an option. The cargo secured in back needed to be delivered without delay, no matter how insane the weather turned, and there was no landing strip for a good hundred miles in any direction. Which basically meant Gabe was an idiot for accepting this job—not that he had a choice.

The landscape ahead looked gray and white—the only visual cues to height and distance was the river below the mountain peaks. Flying at this low altitude was borderline suicidal, but getting caught on radar would put Gabe behind bars. He'd rather take a crazy chance than wear the orange jump suit. He'd rather die than be locked in a cell that would remind him of that cage his partner had rescued him from five years ago.

The nightmares still plagued him.

Gabe squinted to concentrate on the flight path ahead as snow hit the windshield, creating the illusion of a time-warp tunnel.

Flying flowed in his veins. His grandfather and father were distinguished pilots in their own right—Grandpa a fighter pilot in the Second World War, and his father one of the best bush pilots in northern Canada. Neither of them would be proud of what Gabe did for a living, but this was what he did best. He was up in the sky before he could walk and he loved the freedom of being up the air.

"Always fly the plane...never let it fly you," his father always said. Those words had kept Gabe alive on more than one occasion when a flight got out of control.

He chuckled, recalling his last trip to Columbia and the ruckus ditch they'd called a landing strip. The Skyhawk came down on one wheel and skidded across the muddy runway, stopped only by a tree stump in the ground that barely prevented him from going over the hillside cliffs.

Now, as he flew low over the Canadian Rockies, Gabe realized this flight would have been a dangerous mission at any time, never mind during midwinter when his chances of surviving a crash were practically zero. But he lived for reckless adventure, always abiding Colton's demands. Over the years, the more dangerous the job, the more excited he was to take it on.

But as the gray hairs kept growing, and his body continued aching, he wondered if there was more to life than this. More than risking his hide at every turn and living a solitary existence. More than busting his ass for Colton McCoy and his empire. The reckless need for speed and danger had already begun to lessen in his early thirties. If he could get away with it, this would be the last mission. It was high time he put up his feet and enjoyed the money he'd fought hard to earn.

A shift in turbulence made the plane jolt so hard Gabe collided against the dash. He gripped the throttle, keeping the nose level as the engine surged with a loud roar, then eased to a low rumble. Gabe looked down at the instrument panel and blew out a curse when the needles spun out of control.

"Don't do this to me now, baby. Come on," he urged, patting the dash with one hand and pulling the throttle back slightly with the other. The Skyhawk was his baby. They'd been through hell and back on missions some might consider suicidal.

Chinook winds battered the plane, tossing the aircraft around like a dry leaf. Every time he shifted the throttle another gust tossed him in the wrong direction. Left with little choice as the engine sputtered and lost momentum, Gabe opened the side window to view the landscape below.

The river twisted like a snake beneath him, and on each side the towering Rockies left no room for a safe landing.

Strong winds blew snow off the mountains, creating tails of white through the sky, making it impossible to see exactly where the mountain ridges started or ended.

The engine sputtered again before the props stilled. Nothing but the sound of the wind howled through the cockpit.

"Fuck!"

Gabe held the throttle in a pointless death grip. The Cessna was now in the hands of the shifting Canadian winds. There was no time to pray, even for a man who didn't believe in God, and he could not radio "Mayday" and risk the authorities finding him. His life and the cargo were now at the mercy of the wild.

He caught a brief glimpse of snow-covered mountains ahead, before the plane took a nosedive into the white depths below.

Chapter One

Mima Etu angled the dog sled, helping her excited team advance around a dangerous bend in the trail. With one mukluk on the runner, she pedaled with the other, helping the team keep their pace as they climbed the embankment running alongside the river. Her legs trembled, and she sucked in short, sharp breaths from the exertion, but there was no way she'd let Mary win.

Just past dawn, the foggy morning promised a mild day. She filled her lungs with wilderness air, thrilled to be out running so early in the morning. Sledding was food for her soul.

Mima and her best friend, Mary, pushed both teams hard, fighting for the lead along the straightaway, their sleds mere inches from each other. Where Mary had a team of seven small Samoyeds, Mima ran three Siberian huskies and two big Greenlands. Mary's team was quick while Mima's had more power.

"You're out of shape this year," Mary shouted over the jingling sled bells.

"It's the first day of the year, asshole."

They both laughed and pushed their teams harder.

"I'm gonna beat you again," Mary teased, pedaling behind her sled, hustling the dogs along the trail. Her sled picked up momentum and pulled a few yards ahead.

"Like hell. Haw!" Mima's team took the left turn tight around a rock cut, gaining the advantage. They continued quickly along the trail, weaving around snow-covered pines and boulders bordering the river's edge, but on the next straightaway, Mary's team charged forward, leaving Mima in her snowy wake.

Those damn dogs of hers are quick on the line. Mima smiled despite Mary passing her. The woman always gave her a run for her money, and she enjoyed the challenge. One of these days she'd beat her, and then she could rub it back in her face.

"Easy... Easy," she called out to her team. They slowed to a leisurely pace along the trail, allowing Mima the chance to gaze at the surrounding wilderness without distraction.

She loved it out here. This was her life and her home. A sandy beach down south didn't hold a candle to the crisp, white scenery of midwinter on her land. City skyscrapers held no promise of adventure as these towering mountains did. As far as she was concerned, the world outside of this land did not exist.

Her sled—still decorated from the Christmas season—jingled with every bump as the team ascended the foothills toward her home. They struggled up the embankment, panting as they dug their paws into the trail and booked it toward home. The two Greenlands, Musti and Little Red, pulled hard; their job was carrying the weight in the back. Mima hopped off the runners to help ease their burden, but as soon as they crested the hill, the team suddenly halted.

Mima caught her chest on the handlebar, nearly toppling over the sled. "What the hell?"

Mary's team stood silent in the middle of the trail with the brake secured in the snow. Their snouts and ears pointed anxiously toward some unseen presence beyond the trees, while Mary trudged through the deep snow around the bush line.

Mima set her brake in the snow and stepped on it, wondering what had caught her friend's attention.

"What is it?"

Mary waved her arm, gesturing to come closer. "I think it's a plane."

With her stomach in knots, Mima made her way over and halted when she eyed a crumpled blue-and-white Cessna. A sprawling birch jutting up alongside the steep embankment was all that kept the plane from plunging into the river below.

"Do you think that's the plane we heard yesterday evening?"

Mary shrugged. "I don't know, but it looks like a recent crash. What if there's blood and guts in there?" She stared up at Mima, her chin quivering.

After one of Mary's dogs jumped at a spinning plane propeller a few years back, she had nightmares for months and hadn't gone near a plane since. Mima couldn't blame her.

She offered a reassuring smile. "I'll go look. Stay with the dogs before they yank the brakes and take off. They're getting restless."

Mary nodded resolutely and headed back to man the teams.

Eerie silence charged the air as Mima faced the plane, every muscle in her body tight. The plane was so crumpled she couldn't tell if it had wheels or skis.

She pulled herself up to look into the cockpit and gasped. A man lay slumped over the steering wheel, his head leaning against the dashboard. Somehow he had managed to stay in his seat even though he wore no seat belt. His skin appeared gray, and dried blood covered the left side of his face.

"There's a pilot here," Mima shouted. "I think he's dead." Mary's eyes widened. "Did you check his pulse?"

With a trembling hand, Mima reached through the busted window and pressed her fingertips to his throat. The pilot twitched, and she yanked her hand back as if burned. "He's alive! We need to get him out of here fast."

She examined the crumpled pilot door, her mind racing with a plan. "Hang in there, buddy."

The whole right side of the plane was buried deep in the snow, lodged against the birch tree, and the left side must have hit the ground first, which caused it to crumple. As she glanced back at the dogs, an idea suddenly came to her. Using the team's strength to pull the door might be the pilot's only hope.

"Mary, unhook my team and bring them over. I need them to pull the door open."

Mima stayed with the pilot as Mary rushed back to her sled. She removed the gangline connecting the dogs to the sled and secured it to the hook line. Holding Nitchie's collar, Mary then guided the team to the plane. After a few minutes struggling to set them up straight ahead of the door, she tossed Mima the snow hook to wrap around the handle of the pilot door.

Excited and charged-up, the dogs barked and jumped—their instinct ready to pull.

Mima tied the hook end around the door handle. When she was sure the hook would hold, she motioned for Mary to stand by the dogs. "They need to pull hard or this door won't budge."

"Okay." Mary jumped and clapped her hands, revving up the team, and shouted, "Hike hard!"

The team lunged forward, pulling the gangline taut and snapping the crisp air like a whip. Metal creaked and groaned, shifting from the frame as the dogs worked the line. "Hike!" Another hard tug and the door broke away, hurtling into the snow behind the wheel dogs.

"Whoa!" Mary lunged for Nitchie, the lead dog, and grabbed his collar before they took off down the trail without their musher.

"Now for the fun part," Mima said when Mary returned. "He's

not a small guy."

Mary glanced inside. "Maybe if we both take an arm we can pull him out. We're not *that* weak."

Each of them grabbed a shoulder and tugged hard, dragging his limp, heavy body out of the cockpit and onto Mima's sled. They tucked him in tight with the blankets she always had on board. When the hard part was over, the girls both sighed in unison.

Mary stared at the frozen pilot, her face a mask of curious uncertainty. "Should we get him to town?"

If it were a perfect world, this wouldn't have happened to begin with, and even though Mima knew the pilot needed medical assistance, the sun had already begun to set. They'd never make it in time. Sledding at night around here was too dangerous.

She contemplated the best course of action. "It'll be dark soon, and he needs heat. Besides, you still need to make it home too." She looked around the surrounding bush, thinking she didn't want to bring him home where she lived alone. But how dangerous could a half-dead man be? "Let's bring him to my place and see what happens first. I could always radio a rescue chopper in the morning if he needs it."

Mary patted the man's shoulder. "You're lucky we found you, buddy." Then she went back to her sled and yanked her snow hook out of the ground.

"Hike!"

Both teams jumped at the command and surged forward. They maintained a brisk pace, pushing the dogs to the peak of their power and speed. As she pulled away from the crash site, Mima looked back in the direction of the plane. *What was he doing flying alone way out here?* Sure, plane crashes happened often enough, but flying over this area during midwinter was like knocking on death's door. This range of mountains was known for its turbulent winds.

Either the pilot lost direction or he *had* to fly over this area. Either way, he had a rabbit's foot up his ass that she and Mary had taken the old trail today. Otherwise, he would have died out here, alone, in that wreck of a plane.

* * * *

A couple hours later, Mima and Mary stood at the foot of the bed in Mima's cabin. They stared down at the stranger, each one lost in their own thoughts.

"Where do you think he's from?" Mary asked quietly.

"I don't know, but I've never seen a man around here with that many earrings."

Two gold hoops in one ear, and a single diamond stud in the other made the guy look like a rugged gypsy. Wavy, dark brown hair to his broad shoulders matched his five-o'clock shadow. Now that his color had returned—an olive complexion—Mima thought him handsome, even with the jagged scar across his right cheek.

He looked like a modern outlaw.

Too much time had passed since she'd felt attraction to a man, and of course, finding one near dead was the best she could do. "Is it me, or is he one of the finest- looking men you've ever seen?" She bit her lip and glanced over his form.

They'd removed his frozen clothes, leaving only his boxers on, and tucked him under the thickest blankets Mima owned.

"I guess so," Mary said, angling her head to check him out more. "That missing baby toe is a downer though."

The toe could have been lost to frostbite, even though he didn't look like the mountain-climbing type. But the jagged scars all over him? There were so many, Mima stopped counting at twenty. Some were short, thin cuts, or small, circular scars. The others were thick and long as if somebody had whipped him, or slashed at him with a knife. She shuddered at how he must have suffered through all that.

She'd cleaned the blood on his face with a warm washcloth and stitched up the cuts where his head had smashed into the window. Thank goodness her brother had been accident-prone and Mother had taught her what to do. The pilot didn't move an inch as the needle and thread pierced his skin. Either he was seriously out cold or his pain tolerance was impressive.

Anxiety flooded Mima's stomach and she swallowed. The pilot had a body like a hero from an action movie, with thick, corded arms and wide shoulders. A broad chest peppered with dark hair tapered to a narrow waist, all the way down to a set of strong, sculpted legs. Tight boxer briefs stretched taut over the distinct bulge at his crotch. She blew out a shaky breath and blushed, dragging her gaze away from him.

"You thinking what I'm thinking?" Mary's eyes glinted with amusement as she clucked her tongue.

"What?"

"That you're fucking lucky to finally have a man in your bed." Mima laughed, shoving her best friend's shoulder. "The guy's half-dead. Give him a break." Even as she said the words, she couldn't help eyeing him up again.

"Well, I need to get home before it gets dark, or Tom might get worried. Think I should look in the guy's plane and bring by his luggage or whatever personal things he might have in there? He didn't have a wallet on him." Mima shrugged. "That's up to you. He's stuck here for now anyway until I decide what to do with him. So far, I think he's only out from the bump on his head and the cold."

"Poor guy, eh?" Mary gave the pilot a pat on the foot before giving Mima a big hug. "Okay, g'night, babe. Have fun. I'll drop by as soon as I can."

"Radio when you get home, okay?"

"Sure thing, boss." Mary tapped the heels of her boots and saluted her. Mima laughed and gave Mary a friendly push toward the door. The woman was playing a comedienne at the worst time.

Soon her home was quiet, and she stood alone, staring down at the stranger in her bed. He wasn't out of danger yet, and she had a feeling when he woke up there could be more trouble to come.

Meet the Author

Andie J. Christopher writes edgy, funny, sexy contemporary romance. She grew up in a family of voracious readers, and picked up her first Harlequin romance novel at age twelve when she'd finished reading everything else in her grandmother's house. It was love at first read. It wasn't too long before she started writing her own stories—her first heroine drank Campari and wore a lot of Esprit. Andie holds a bachelor's degree from the University of Notre Dame in economics and art history (summa cum laude), and a JD from Stanford Law School. She lives in Washington, DC, with a very funny French Bulldog named Gus. Please visit her at andiejchristopher.com.

Lightning Source UK Ltd.
Milton Keynes UK
UKHW012003010920
369187UK00001B/25